MURPHY MURPHY
AND THE CASE
OF SERIOUS CRISIS

Pulled from the files of the
Department of Redundancy Department

Keith Hirshland

BEACON

For information, or to order additional copies,
please contact:

Beacon Publishing Group
P.O. Box 41573 Charleston, S.C. 29423
800.817.8480| beaconpublishinggroup.com

Publisher's catalog available by request.

ISBN-13: 978-1-949472-12-7

ISBN-10: 1-949472-12-7

Published in 2020. New York, NY 10001.

First Edition. Printed in the USA.

"Never put the cart before the horse/
Unless he knows how to push it, of course"

Pat Green

A long slender finger pressed the button, popping the car's trunk. The nail was in decent shape, but the cuticle, recently gnawed, displayed the slightest bit of dried blood. A pair of scuffed Doc Martens hit the pavement, left foot first, and headed to the back of the automobile.

A Caran d'Ache Carbon fiber lighter was tossed into the trunk, landing on top of a black, pebbled leather motorcycle jacket. Next to the jacket lay a whip; nine foot by twelve, plait, black and tan, made from kangaroo hide. Near the whip were other items including, but not limited to, a Brackish brand bird feather bow tie; a Code 38 stealth titanium corkscrew; an eight pack of La Croix Pamplemousse sparkling water and a dozen Titleist Pro V1 golf balls.

The driver surveyed the booty in the boot, and with both hands slammed the trunk shut.

THE STORY BEGINS

Murphy Murphy stood under the steady stream of hot water pouring from the shower head for a few minutes longer than normal. He closed his eyes and gave thought to his paternal lineage, from great great grandfather down. They were all Murphy Murphy's, and they were all cops.

Another characteristic of Murphy progeny was that the men, after marriage, sired one, and only one, male offspring. A lad that, tradition held, would be named Murphy. They fathered girls as well, of course, as many as they wanted or could afford. But only first. Once a baby boy, a male Murphy, was christened into the world, the baby making stopped. As you can imagine, that placed an inordinate amount of pressure on each and every Murphy to continue the family bloodline. Most made quick work of the obligation by marrying young and getting right to work at keeping the line moving. Most, but not all. The currently soaking wet Murphy Murphy seemed to be thumbing his nose at the family custom, having recently celebrated his 31st birthday as a bachelor.

No Murphy Murphy's had brothers, but this Murphy Murphy had a sister who was, as another family ritual dictated, named Muffy. This Murphy's Muffy rebelled, ran away from home, changed her name to Lisa Lisa, then formed a rock and roll band. As the water started to cool, Murphy Murphy thought of her and hummed her number one hit, "Lost in Emotion".

THE STORY CONTINUES

Murphy wrapped the towel around his waist and slid his size eleven feet into a brand-new pair of navy, Nappa leather slippers. They looked just like the ones he remembered running up the stairs to get whenever Grandpa Murphy Murphy, and later his own "Pops", Murphy Murphy, asked for them. He knew for a fact great Grandpa Murphy Murphy had a similar pair as well. He'd heard stories of his Grandmother's scolding cries about the "waste of a hard earned two dollars and ninety cents!" The memory made him smile; he only wished his modern day "house shoe" indulgence cost so little. All clean, with tootsies warm and cozy, he grabbed his phone. A red dot indicated he had missed one call.

"Murph," Murphy heard the voice say the nickname he disliked. Truth be told he didn't really mind the abbreviated version of his given name, he just resented the fact that his captain frequently used it. "Captain Hill here. I need you back at the precinct bright and early tomorrow." Murphy Murphy was a seven-year veteran of the force and, as of now, the only member of the recently formed Department of Redundancy Department at the cop shop. The irony, while oblivious to some, was obvious to Detective Murphy Murphy. He hit the pause button on the phone and rolled his eyes.

At the Captain's request he had stayed late that night copyreading and editing the paperwork that was scheduled to be filed by other officers and detectives. Captain Hill liked clean, concise reports and he knew Murphy was a stickler for good grammar. Murphy hoped the additional hours spent at work might translate into a little extra shuteye the next day. Clearly that was not meant to be. He hit the play icon and the message picked up where he had left it off.

"I've got something special for you, pal. A case that, I think, is right up your alley. Let's say I see you standing at attention, in front of my desk, at 8 AM in the morning." There it was. Murphy Murphy cringed after hearing the redundancy even though he knew it was coming. Captain Hill was well aware of Murphy's aversion to redundant phrases. In fact, Hill took particular glee in telling everyone who would listen that the young detective "hated them with a passion" and he made every effort to use as many of them as he could think of around Murphy Murphy. The Captain had made his mocking abundantly transparent at the outset. When telling Murphy of his promotion and new assignment the Captain added, with a smirk, "I debated giving you a partner but figured, considering the caseload, that would be," he paused for effect, "redundant."

"Jerk," Murphy practically spat as he deleted the message. Then he kicked off his slippers, shed the towel, pulled down his Murphy bed, and called it a night.

THE STORY STILL CONTINUES

It wasn't as much as he had hoped, but Murphy Murphy did get a few extra minutes of sleep thanks to the late shower the night before. He recently had the barber cut his hair short so he could make his morning grooming less time consuming. She called it a buzz cut. He remembered wondering, during the process, if the "buzz" was in reference to the length of the hair that would remain on his head or the sound the clipper made when it mowed the follicles down. He decided he didn't care.

He rubbed deodorant into his pits, brushed his teeth and put on his uniform. In stockinged feet, he padded to the kitchen where he tossed some tropical fruit into a blender, then added coconut milk, a little kale, protein powder, and some chia seeds. He hit the power button and thirty seconds later had breakfast. The last thing he did was put on and lace his expertly shined shoes before he headed out the door, making the ten-minute walk to the police station in eight. As a result, he was a few minutes early, so he checked the phone on his desk for any overnight calls. Seeing there were none, he then headed upstairs. Per the message from the night before he, stood at attention in front of the Captain's desk.

Captain David "DUD" Hill read the nameplate at the exact center of the desktop; gold letters on a black lacquer plate. It may have struck the uninformed as a strange, if not downright demeaning, nickname. Certainly not a moniker any right-thinking person would embrace. But Murphy Murphy was anything but uninformed. He knew exactly why Dave Hill was "Dud" to his closest friends and why he went by it so proudly. To kill some time, Murphy rolled the story over in his head.

As a uniformed patrolman, while off duty shopping at the mall, Officer David Hill came across a suspicious looking package sitting unattended in front of a popular chain coffee store. The joint was packed. A line of people, willing to spend six bucks on a cup of joe, stretched well out the entrance and reached into the common area of the mall. The parcel couldn't have looked more out of place. It was actually a medium-sized, brand new black duffle bag. The tags, from the nearby luggage and personal pocket knife store, were still attached. As the curious officer took two steps past it, he got a closer look at the price tag and asked himself why someone would leave a brand spanking new duffle bag on the ground in front of a coffee store. He took a couple more steps before he stopped, turned, and doubled back, fully intending to take the bag inside the store for safe keeping. He reasoned the purchaser would surely realize he or she had left an item of such expense behind and return to claim it. Before picking it up he peeked inside.

What he saw sent a chill down his spine. Sticks of what he was sure was dynamite were bound together with black electrical tape. There was other paraphernalia his mind didn't immediately catalogue because he was focused on a digital clock that displayed a countdown already at ten seconds. Dave Hill had no practical experience with explosives, but he surmised what he had here was a bomb and, if the clock was correct, it was about to go off. So he did what he thought every uniformed member of the police force and each invested citizen of the community would do. He screamed at the top of his lungs, "EVERYBODY GET DOWN!" and dove on top of the bag hoping his 270-pound frame would mitigate some, if not all, of the collateral damage. He didn't pray, he didn't think, he didn't breathe. He simply waited to be blown to bits. Seconds that felt like hours, past the allotted ten, went by and Officer Dave Hill was still in one piece. Instead of feeling an explosion underneath him he felt a hand on his back and heard a voice above him.

"Hey buddy, you okay?" Hill turned his head slightly and saw a pair of black, scuffed, Bates brand high shine patrol oxfords. He recognized the brand because he owned two pair of his own. His were spit shined and flawless. Another second without an explosion went by and Hill realized that he was looking at the feet of a shopping center security guard.

"Bomb," he said simply. "Call 9-1-1."

"Excuse me?" the mall cop leaned from his ample waist, "What did you say?"

"I said bomb. I'm lying on top of a bomb! Now call 9-1-1 dumbass!"

"No need to be rude, pal," The security guard answered defensively. "And, more correctly, you're the one lying on top of a bomb, so who, exactly, is the *dumbass,*" he added. Then he called it in.

It turned out David Hill had indeed uncovered a bomb. It's just that this device wasn't particularly well made. The would-be bomber turned out to be a women's shoe salesman at one of the mall's anchor stores who had made the device in order to "send a message" to the coffee chain.

"I was sick and tired of them burning the espresso beans," he had told a member of the S.W.A.T. team that led him away in cuffs.

"Just wait until you taste the joe in the hoosegow," the cop had replied with a disgusted laugh.

The problem with the shoe salesman's bomb was that he had failed to hook the timer up to the explosive device so there was never a chance of it exploding. Its only future was to be a dud, but Officer David Hill had no way of knowing that when he made his heroic decision to sacrifice his own life to save as many others as he could. The young cop didn't get blown up, but he did move up. There was a promotion, a parade, free coffee (that he didn't drink) for the rest of his life, a key to the city, and a nickname. "Dud". Now he was a Captain in the police department and destined to be Chief. He was also, at the moment, standing in his office door, behind Murphy Murphy.

"I could have guessed you'd be here early," the Captain said, "Unfortunately, something important has come up and this meeting will have to be postponed until later." The Captain suppressed a laugh while Murphy bit his lip. Then he spun one hundred and eighty degrees and wordlessly walked past the Captain and out the door. His face reddened as he heard bellows of laughter behind him. He made his way toward the stairs and down to his office in the basement of the building.

Murphy Murphy sat behind his desk and stewed. He'd heard all the stories and knew what his Captain had done. Risking his own life to save others. But in Murphy's mind, that didn't give the man the right to be a complete and utter plonker. It wasn't an excuse to, carte blanche, purposely belittle another human being, especially a brother in blue. In public or in private, for that matter.

"Especially," he said out loud to the picture of the current POTUS hanging on his wall, "when the obnoxious behavior is at the expense of the rules of grammar." He shook his head slowly, sadly, then added, "A lawman should show more respect."

"Murph!" the voice of Captain Hill crackled through the tiny speaker on his phone. "Got a minute." It wasn't a question

"On my way, Cap," he answered. And he was.

"Thanks for coming up so quickly," the Captain addressed his detective as soon as Murphy walked through the door. On the way, he wondered how many redundant phrases his superior officer would lob in his direction during this particular meeting. Of course, the length of the meeting always had some bearing on that figure. He put the over/under prediction at five.

"The reason why," the Captain started.

"One," Murphy Murphy said under his breath.

"I needed to talk to you at the present time."

That's a quick two, thought Murphy, starting to get ticked off.

"I have a case for you." Murphy's ears perked up as a sense of excitement came over him. It always did when he was faced with the prospect of real police work. "Allow me to spell it out for you in detail," the Captain added.

"Three," counted Murphy Murphy through the excitement.

AT THE SAME EXACT TIME

DeMaio Turrell opened his right eye. Thanks to a reflected image from a mirrored ceiling, it appeared that his left eye was staring back. He was alone in the round bed; one leg outside the covers, the other underneath. It took him several seconds to put the pieces of where he was together. *Hotel room; Across from the arena; Big show last night; Decent after party*. The staccato thoughts raced through his brain. He also remembered that he had company when he returned to the hotel. He found and checked his phone, the display telling him it was still before noon. *Early* he thought as he rolled out of the bed and headed to the bathroom.

Turrell was the popular lead singer and front man for the band Serious Crisis. Born Walter Ames Turrell, he was named for his great grandfather. W. A. Turrell the elder, started his professional life as a lawyer and ended it as a New Hampshire State Supreme Court Justice. Walter the younger grew up hating his name and all the Wally's, Walt's, and W. A.'s that came with it. His grandparents were lawyers. His mother and father were lawyers. He had two older sisters, both attorneys, and it was expected young Walter Ames would toe the line. His grades were good in

14

high school, certainly good enough to get "legacied" into Columbia where he lasted exactly two-thirds of one semester.

He had no interest following in his family's footsteps and practicing law. He loved music and wanted nothing more than to write songs, sing them, and play them on his guitar. His parents were disappointed but stopped short of disowning the boy completely. Their chagrin, however, didn't stop them from cutting off any and all support. While disillusioned with them, Walt didn't care all that much because his maternal grandmother loved the fact that "little Wally" wanted to be an artist and, unbeknownst to her daughter and her daughter's husband, she became her grandson's greatest advocate and benefactor.

Walter left Morningside Heights and moved to Chicago to chase his dream. He wrote music and lyrics and talked his way into singing for his supper at a number of bars, restaurants, and coffee houses. He made ends meet working as a delivery guy for a local sandwich shop. Before getting the job and risking his life by riding his bike around the windy city distributing subs, he frequented the operation and ate there himself. For lunch, for dinner, sometimes even for breakfast. Every time the same thing; turkey, American cheese, lettuce and tomato on a pretzel baguette. Hold the mayo. He ordered the sandwich so many times his presence in the little shop became legendary. After a little more than a month he was no longer Walter or Walt or Wally; he was "hold the mayo" and eventually, then always, simply "da mayo". Walt liked the nickname, then loved it, then changed it ever so slightly and adopted it.

One of the kids who often made his sandwiches was also a musician and he and "DeMaio" Turrell became more than coworkers. They became friends, then partners in a band. They recruited a few more members, got good, got gigs, made friends in the robust Chicago music scene, and eventually got a record deal. They settled on the name Serious Crisis and the right time, right place, right attitude, right chemistry and a ton of talent added up to a certain amount of stardom and a worldwide following. Turrell's parents never completely absolved their son for rejecting the family's profession and embarking on a divergent career path. But during one recent family Christmas gathering Walter Ames "DeMaio" Turrell snuck into his father's study and found, steeled away in an oak cabinet, the entire *Serious Crisis* catalogue. Even the first record that was met with a fair share of critical ambivalence.

Turrell finished his business on the hotel bathroom toilet and wandered back into the bedroom section of the suite. He recalled rolling a joint the night before and sharing a little more than half of it with his companion. He found what was left in an ashtray next to the bed and meant to finish it for breakfast.

What he couldn't find was his lighter. A sense of panic crept through him, not because of the delay in imbibing the cannabis (which he felt was as good as advertised), but because he couldn't find the incendiary device. He was panicked because it was a Caran d'Ache Carbon Fiber lighter, an $1,800 gift he had presented to himself on his 31st birthday last May. He grabbed his phone again and punched in a number.

"Goosh," he listened as the band's manager acknowledged the call. "I got a problem."

"I'm on it," Jeff Giucigiu, pronounced "goo-she-goo", announced after listening for a minute or two. He ended the conversation with the band's enigmatic, talented, and frustratingly compulsive lead singer.

"What did you expect would happen?" he said into the phone, even though Turrell was no longer on the other end. "You buy a two thousand dollar lighter, then leave it out in the open while you pass out "entertaining" a groupie in your hotel suite!" He shook his head. "I'm surprised that's the only thing that's missing." He would have loved to scold the Serious Crisis front man for real but he liked his job too much. He finished his one-sided conversation and hit the recall button on his phone, realizing he needed to start a two-sided one.

"Walt," he said, using the singer's given name when Turrell picked up.

"Yes Jeff," he replied, annoyed that real names were spoken.

"Is anything else missing?"

"Whaddaya mean?"

"Besides your lighter. Is anything else gone?"

"Don't know. Didn't get that far. I'll look."

"You do that, okay DeMaio?"

"Will do Goosh." Giucigiu disconnected and plopped down on the sofa in his own sweet suite. He looked out the 27th floor window and admired the big city skyline. The band was in the middle of a lengthy tour in support of its latest release, *Ascend Up the Ladder*. It was an exhausting ritual; hitting the stage at night, boarding the tour bus the next day and rolling down the road to the next arena filled with tens of thousands of screaming fans. As demanding and time consuming as touring was, Jeff Giucigiu never tired of the life. He loved the energy each crowd released and marveled at how his friends had the ability to turn that energy into an enthusiastic performance every night. The group, together for nearly a decade, had recently found another gear, another level of creativity and force. The manager put that square on the shoulders of the newest member of Serious Crisis; guitarist, keyboardist, and back-up singer, Lyndsay Howlund.

She joined Serious Crisis in the months when *Ascend Up the Ladder* was being recorded. She injected a much-needed shot of energy into the group and her song, "Fewer in Number", became the group's first bona fide Billboard Magazine number one hit. She was as smart as she was talented, and she brought a sense of civility to the rest of the band. She helped transform the frat boy culture, by which the band had operated, into a family. The success of her song, and their record, turned Serious Crisis into a serious business. This most recent tour schedule included several breaks. One, two, or even three days off between gigs so everyone could recharge their batteries, see the sights, do laundry or reconnect with loved ones. Nobody was married, but some had significant others and they all had parents and family members, including Lyndsay Howlund whose uncle just happened to be the Captain of a Police Department.

Giucigiu thought about Turrell's lighter and wondered if other items belonging to the lead singer were no longer in his possession. It made him curious if other members of Serious Crisis had discovered personal objects missing. He grabbed his phone again and pounded out ten numbers.

"Hey Jeff." Lyndsay was the only person who routinely called the manager by his first name. He liked that.

"Hey stray dog," Giucigiu used the nickname he and the band's drummer Herbie Albanese had given Howlund when she showed up at the group's hotel one night. "I think it's time for a team meeting." Then he asked for her help in getting the band together.

THE STORY TURNS BACK TO MURPHY AND CONTINUES TO CONTINUE

After work Murphy walked home, despite the fact that Captain Hill had, months ago, assigned him a police vehicle. The car was a 1985 Renault Le Car. Like many things that pertained to his detective, Murphy Murphy, the Captain thought assigning that particular vehicle was hilarious. The car was boldly yellow with a black racing stripe. The words **Le Car** were printed just below the stripe on both the driver's and passenger's doors. The department had added **of the DRD** (short for of the Department of Redundancy Department) right after **Le Car**. In Murphy's mind, the less time he spent behind the wheel of that vehicle, the better.

In his apartment he changed out of his uniform and slipped on a t-shirt and a pair of shorts. After finding, then sliding into, a pair of flip flops, he left the house again, walking equidistance the other way from work along the sidewalk. He passed a newsstand, paid two bucks for the local paper, and kept going past a battery store, a mobile phone provider, and his least favorite restaurant. It was an Italian joint called Restaurant Trattoria and he had long since vowed to never darken its door. After walking by a narrow alley littered with an inordinate number of half full dumpsters and occupied by the block's lone homeless person, Murphy reached his destination.

Bar Flight was his "go to" establishment. The joint was owned by a former boxer, a local legend named Richie Pizzoni. A national sportswriter had nicknamed the middleweight "The Pizzer" after a colleague had remarked, "that ol' Dick sure can let loose a steady stream of rights and lefts!" The subsequent cover of the sport's most-read trade magazine featured a picture of the newly crowned champ lording over his victim with the words: "Richie "The Pizzer" Pizzoni Takes the Belt."

Between rounds of most fights, Richie would daydream of one day getting out of the fight game and opening up a bar in his old neighborhood. It turned out holding one middleweight title was cache enough to make that happen. So that was the first *and* last time "The Pizzer" graced the cover of *Boxing Times*. He wanted to name the place Bar Fight but the town elders, three of which were octogenarian grandmothers, wrinkled their collective noses at that idea. So Pizzoni went back a month later, this time represented by a lawyer, who suggested Bar Flight instead.

"You know, like a flight of expensive wines," Richie piped up, even though the elders were well aware what a "flight" was.

The committee loved it, thinking it struck the perfect note of sophistication, and approved the license on the spot. Not more than a month after opening night the neon *"l"* in the sign serendipitously went down for the count and "The Pizzer" ended up becoming the proud owner of a place called "Bar Fight" after all. Buck, the bouncer, had been Richie's sparring partner. Before that he was an opponent in the opposite corner of the ring. During one fight, thanks to a particularly impressive flurry, Richie's fists became the reason Buck needed an orthodontist and a new occupation. The champ figured the least he could do was give the guy a job or two.

Out of politeness and habit, Murphy Murphy wiped his feet at the bar's doorstep and went inside. He nodded at Buck who greeted him formally.

"Welcome back Mr. Murphy," Buck grunted through a mouthful of fake teeth. They were the same four words Buck said to Murphy every time he walked through the door. Except, of course, the very first time Murphy Murphy walked through the door.

"Evening Buck," Murphy replied.

He strolled between the two pool tables, currently unoccupied, and stopped, waiting for a dart to go whistling past his left ear. Coast clear, he continued and saddled up to the bar. A double Jameson Irish whiskey, looking all golden and delicious, was waiting there for him.

"Hey Jude," he said to a woman behind the bar. She was facing the bottles, not the customers.

"Hey Murphy," she said back. "How was your day?"

"Big day," Murphy said only half joking. "I got these," he offered as he pushed a standard sized business card across the bar before gulping down two fingers worth of the whiskey. The woman turned and faced him with a big, welcoming, smile. Judith Colman ran the bar and had since the second week Bar Flight opened. Richie wanted to tend bar himself but he couldn't make what he called "the fancy drinks" and, instead of learning, he got mad at the customers when they ordered them.

Murphy Murphy had never seen Judith get mad at anybody. She seemed to like everybody, but Murphy soon came to learn she didn't like anybody or anything as much as she did her rescue dogs. She had two, that Murphy knew of, Namath and Bear (she was a University of Alabama graduate) were currently minding their own business behind the bar. If Murphy thought about it, he figured Judith Colman was probably his best friend in the whole world. But when Murphy thought about it, he realized he didn't think about it that much. When he first walked into Pizzoni's establishment and pulled up a stool in front of her bar she had said, "Hello" and asked him his name.

"Murphy Murphy," he answered without hesitation, fully prepared for whatever came next. Usually it was a snicker, a guffaw or an outright laugh accompanied by a "you're kidding" or a smart aleck crack. Judith said nothing. She just turned and grabbed a bottle of Jameson and poured a double. She would later tell Murphy that she simply figured "a nice-looking guy with two good Irish names deserved a double helping of Irish whiskey." Murphy Murphy never asked for anything else. Judith picked the business card up off the bar. It was a standard size, police department issue, replete with seal and all. Smack dab in the center, printed in bold black ink, she could read **Detective Murphy Murphy**. Directly below those three words she saw four more. **Department of Redundancy Department**.

"Very impressive," she claimed

"Keep it," he offered. "I've got a thousand of 'em."

"That's very generous of you." She smiled and slipped the card into the back right pocket of her jeans.

"Oh," Murphy perked up, "and I got a new case." He slapped the bar with his right palm for emphasis.

"New cards need a new case," she teased with

another smile. Murphy rolled his eyes in response. "Congrats Murphy," she said. "Tell me about it." She took a sip from Murphy's glass while he did.

"It was around 11 o'clock," Murphy recalled the events from earlier, "and I had just been summoned to the principal's office." Murphy smiled as he recalled the meeting.

MEANWHILE, THE BAND HAD GATHERED TOGETHER TO MEET WITH EACH OTHER

"Thanks for coming on such short notice," the band's manager said from his spot in the middle of the room.

"Did we have a choice?" It was the group's bass guitar player, "Big Joe" Lionns. Sitting cross-legged on the floor, Lyndsay Howlund shot the questioner a dirty look. "Sorry," he said sheepishly, sitting down on the arm of the sofa.

"What's up Goosh?" Turrell spoke next, "New stop on the tour?"

"Has *Ascend Up the Ladder* gone double platinum?" Herbie Albanese raised his hand and shouted the question.

"You don't have to raise your hand, Herbie," Turrell scolded the drummer.

"Are we finally getting a new tour bus?" That question came from guitarist and Serious Crisis co-founder Chuckie Gruber.

"What's wrong with the tour bus?" Herbie started to raise his hand, then brought it down.

"Nothing if you're short enough to fit in the bunks," Gruber said shaking his head.

"Guys, guys, guys!" Howlund jumped up and faced her band mates. "Enough. Why don't we just let Jeff, er Goosh, tell us why he's called us all together."

"Thanks, Lynds," the manager said, "I'll keep it short and sweet."

"Amen to that."

"Joe. Zip it," Lyndsay scolded the bassist. Turrell giggled.

"It's come to my attention," Jeff continued, "that a piece of personal property, belonging to one of us, has gone missing." The members of the band looked at one another.

"Did one of you nitwits swipe my lighter?" Turrell asked.

"The Carne d'Ache?" Gruber was horrified.

"The Carny day what?" Herbie raised his hand.

"Who would bother swiping a lighter?" Lionns wondered out loud, "they're a dime a dozen."

"This one was more like 18,000 dimes," Gruber replied, still aghast. Herbie Albanese tried to do the math in his head.

"GUYS!" It was Howlund.

"DeMaio's lighter is MIA," Giucigiu tried to regain control of the room. "And nobody thinks anybody in the band, in this room," he made sure to include himself in the absolution, "had anything to do with it."

"But somebody did." This time Herbie didn't raise his hand.

"Somebody did," Giucigiu agreed.

"This is not a forum for accusation," Lyndsay interjected, "It's a simple fact-finding mission."

"That's correct," the manager added. "Now, has anyone else noticed something of yours that's gone AWOL?" Herbie looked around the room quizzically.

"It means 'absent without leave' Herbie," Turrell put a reassuring hand on the drummer's shoulder. "Goosh wants to know if anything you own is gone."

"As a matter of fact..." began Big Joe. As he spoke, other hands went up.

BACK AT BAR FLIGHT, MURPHY MURPHY WASN'T COMPLETELY FINISHED

"So, it turns out," Murphy went on, "my boss, Captain Hill.

"Dud," Judith interrupted

"Pardon?" Murphy stopped

"Dud," she repeated, "Your boss. Captain Hill. Dud." She explained. "Everybody knows who he is and everybody calls him that."

"Not everybody," Murphy took another gulp of whiskey. "Anyway," he started again, "My boss, Captain Hill," Judith smiled and shook her head, "has a niece who's in a rock and roll band."

"Really?" Judith interrupted again, "What band?"

"What?" Murphy looked at her, suddenly exasperated.

"What's the name of the band?" she asked, genuinely curious. Murphy, realizing she was being earnest in her interest, took a deep, cleansing, breath.

"Serious Crisis," he answered. Judith laughed out loud.

"For reals?" she wondered, "Or is Dud yanking your chain?" Murphy Murphy had told his bartender friend about the Captain's penchant for having a laugh at Murphy's expense.

"I wondered that too," he admitted, "but Serious Crisis is an actual band and Captain Hill's niece is a member." He pulled his phone from his pocket. "Says here she plays the keyboard, the guitar, and sings."

"And she wrote "Fewer in Number". Multi-talented," Judith said admiringly as Murphy brought up one of the band's music videos on his mobile. He hit the play icon and noise poured out of the device.

"That's the song." She started bobbing her head up and down, "Been playing on Pandora for weeks." On the floor, one of the rescue dogs, Murphy figured it was Namath, began to howl. "I know, right boy?" she reached down and scratched the dog's head, "We love this song."

Murphy hit the pause icon on his phone and the bobbing and howling stopped. "I believe it's the first hit single off their record *Ascend Up the Ladder*."

"It is, but I don't think they call them records anymore, Murphy," Judith's smile was impossible to miss.

"Whatever," Murphy dismissed her with a wave, "Captain says that song was the band's *major breakthrough.* "

"I bet you loved that description," she said sympathetically.

"You know I did."

"So, what's the case? "She steered the conversation back to its original purpose.

"You want my words or the Captain's?"

"I like yours better."

"The band is currently on tour and visiting seventeen cities in a dozen states. About a third of the way through, possessions belonging to individual members and the band as a whole started disappearing."

"Expensive things?" she asked, her chin resting on cupped hands. Her elbows were on the bar. Her face was right in front of Murphy Murphy's. He looked directly into her baby blue eyes.

"Some," he said

"That's weird," she admitted, "but why does it fall under your jurisdiction?" She asked the same question Murphy had asked his Captain earlier that day.

"Captain Hill said and allow me to quote him now. 'I realize it's a difficult dilemma', unquote." Murphy practically spat out the last two words. "Quote, 'But the kid's mom, my sister, asked me to look into it. Sadly, my docket is completely full.' Again, Murphy nearly choked on the phrase but he composed himself and continued. "Again I quote, 'So you're the next best option to get to the bottom of this unsolved mystery', unquote". Murphy took a long swig of the whisky as if to wash his mouth clean of the offending remarks.

"I guess that all amounts to a compliment," Judith said, refilling his glass.

"It does?" Murphy was clearly unsure.

"Absolutely," She said with another smile. "He's trusting you with his sister's kid's problem. So, where do you start?"

"Seems like the beginning is the best place," he answered. "The Captain gave me the name and number of the band's manager. I guess I should give him a call."

"I guess you do," Judith agreed, walking away.

"See ya Jude."

"See ya Murphy."

Before heading home, he stopped at the door.

"How're you doing Buck?" he asked the bouncer.

"Hangin in," Buck replied, "makin sure trouble hangs out." He added throwing a thumb over his shoulder toward the night. Murphy wondered if "trouble" had ever seen the inside of Bar Flight. He, in fact, had wondered that same question aloud to Richie Pizzoni once, asking why the bar needed a full-time bouncer.

"I've been coming here for months," Murphy Murphy mentioned to "the Pizzer". Richie just looked at Murphy so he kept going, "Is Buck necessary?"

"How do you mean?" the owner had asked

"Well, what I mean is, I've never seen anybody in here looking to raise a ruckus."

"The Pizzer" nodded, then said simply, "Then I guess my bouncer is doing a heck of a job." Murphy couldn't argue with that logic.

"Hey Buck," Murphy had thought of something. "Have you ever heard of Serious Crisis?" Buck furrowed his brow and scratched his chin while thinking hard for a moment.

"What weight class did he fight in?" Buck asked. Murphy smiled.

"Never mind." He patted Buck on the shoulder. "You doing okay? Need anything?"

"Things vacillate back and forth," Buck answered, "but overall I can't complain. What was the second question?" A frequently forgetful Buck had forgotten.

"Can I get you anything?" Murphy asked, carefully using different words.

"Nope." Buck shook his head. "Unless," he paused briefly and Murphy instinctively leaned closer, "you happen to have a shoebox full of hundreds handy." Murphy assured him he did not and walked out of the bar.

THE BAND WAS STILL COLLABORATING TOGETHER

"So, you're missing a bow tie." The manager looked at Big Joe.

"Not just any bow tie," the big man elaborated, "A Brackish Hemlock. That's two hundred and fifty bucks worth of neckwear."

"A two hundred and fifty dollar bow tie?" Turrell sounded dumbfounded

"Don't judge man," Lionns scolded his friend, "It's made of rooster, chukka, and pheasant feathers. A hundred of them."

"Impressive," Turrell had to admit

"And you can't find your brand-new corkscrew." Giucigiu reclaimed the conversation as his gaze shifted to Chuckie Gruber. "Anybody else?" Giucigiu looked around the room. For a handful of seconds, the members of the band looked at each other, the ceiling, their shoes and each other again. Then slowly, sheepishly, Albanese raised his hand.

"You don't have to raise your hand Herbie," an exasperated DeMaio Turrell chastised.

"It's okay Herbie." Lyndsay was much more sympathetic, "What did you lose?"

"I didn't *lose* anything," the drummer said defensively, "Cuz now I know it was swiped." His face reddened.

"What was?" the band's manager asked

"My whip," Herbie said under his breath.

"Your *what?*" Big Joe wondered out loud.

"What did he say?" echoed Gruber

"One more time Herbie," Turrell demanded. "Louder this time," he added. Herbie hung his head and cleared his throat.

"My whip is gone."

"Did you say your whip?" Gruber sounded impressed.

"Geez. Your whip," Joe pointed his finger at Herbie then tucked it in and used his thumb to gesture toward Lyndsay, "And her balls," he shook his head. "What kind of band is this?"

"A fun one," said a smiling Turrell.

"Wait a sec." It was Giucigiu. "Did you say her *balls?*" The manager pointed at Howlund.

"I did," Big Joe nodded.

"He did," Lyndsay confirmed. "It's just I was certain that I had another dozen Titleist Pro V1's," she added.

"X's?" Turrell asked with more than a hit of envy in his voice.

"Nope," Howlund answered, "Just the Pro V's. I like the way they feel around the greens." Turrell nodded his approval. "I was sure I had five dozen, but when I went to play the other day, I could only find four. I just assumed DeMaio helped himself," Lyndsay shrugged.

"Hey!" Turrell shot back. "Not a chance Chicka. I play the Chrome Soft just like my boy Phil Mickelson."

"You sure you didn't lose them on the golf course?" Lionns asked condescendingly.

"Lose a dozen balls? And not remember?" she responded. "That's impossible."

"Not for Big Joe." It was Turrell again.

Big Joe's rejoinder was the middle finger of his left hand. Everybody got a good laugh. Everybody but Herbie Albanese, that is.

"It's a tool," Herbie said defensively, still lamenting the loss of his whip. "Remember when we were touring with the Crab Apples?" he asked. Some nodded. "Their drummer John Paul Oldham,"

"The Pope!" Big Joe screamed. "I loved that guy."

"He was a good guy, for sure," Herbie agreed. "He was also a great drummer." Everybody in the room nodded this time. "Well, between sets one night we were talking about the sweet science."

"I believe the sweet science refers to boxing," Giucigiu interrupted.

"Not if you ask drummers," Herbie countered confidently.

"Fair enough," the manager acquiesced.

"Now, where was I? Oh yeah, me and the pope were talking drumming."

"The pope and I." This time the interruption came from Howlund.

"For God's sake!" Herbie stood, arms outstretched. "Can I just please finish my story?!"

"Depends," Howlund replied with a straight face.

"Go ahead Herb," Turrell prompted

"Thanks Walter," Herbie nodded in the lead singer's direction. He received a dirty look in return. "I mean DeMaio." Turrell smiled. "So, the pope and I," he looked at Lyndsay, "were talking drumming and he said one of the ways he stayed in shape was with a whip. Good for the wrists, he said, so I took his advice and bought one. A nice one," he added proudly.

"You *are* killing it back there lately," Chuckie Gruber gave a shout out to the band's drummer.

"Where the heck did you find a whip?" Big Joe asked. "A nice one," he added.

"Online," he responded. "Isn't that where everybody finds everything?"

"Okay." It was the manager again, "Good story there Herbie, now let's recap. DeMaio lost a lighter."

"Uh, no Jeff, it was *stolen*," the lead singer was quick to clarify.

"Right. That's what I meant." The manager tried to continue.

"But that's not what you *said*."

"Fair enough. I apologize. Let me start over. A lighter is missing."

"Stolen."

"So is a whip." This time the manager didn't indulge the Serious Crisis front man. "Also, a bow tie, a corkscrew and a dozen golf balls." Everyone in the band looked at everyone else. "It would appear this is a case of *band*itry." The manager stopped,

40

expecting a reaction. He got none. "Get it? *BAND*itry? Emphasis on the *band?*" Still nothing from the room. "Never mind," he continued, "And it seems to have affected each and every one of us."

"Except you," Big Joe pointed a long index finger at Giucigiu.

"Well…" the manager responded, "I'm pretty darn sure I used to have one more eight pack of La Croix pamplemousse."

KNOWING HE WASN'T IN GRAVE PERIL, MURPHY MURPHY DID WHAT HE ALWAYS DID AND WALKED HOME FROM THE BAR

On the way home Murphy crossed the deserted street and popped into the convenience store on the block. It was called The Triangle and, because it was actually a rectangle, Murphy Murphy always wondered why whoever named it named it so. Once upon a time he thought to ask, but these days he no longer cared. A small bell rang, announcing his presence as he opened the door. He headed to the back of the store where the cold beverages were on display. He'd had his fill of alcohol for the evening, since two Jamesons was his limit on most nights and he wasn't looking for more. What he wanted, needed, because he was out of it, was water. But not just any water. He was after The Mountain Valley Spring Water.

Murphy had stumbled upon the Arkansas sourced H20 a few years back and now found it difficult to drink any other brand. He convinced Pratik, the Triangle's owner, to stock the beverage with the promise that he would make it worth his while. A five hundred dollar cash advance sealed the deal. It wasn't that the tap water in town was bad, it was awful. Most importantly, Murphy Murphy discovered that The Mountain Valley Spring Water, at forty bucks per twenty-four bottles, made an absolutely exquisite cup of Darjeeling.

"Evening Mr. Double M squared," Pratik's son Pravit addressed Murphy from behind the counter.

"That's too many M's," Murphy said out of repetition more than anything. The teaching moment had long since passed.

"Out of water?" Pravit asked, despite having to have already known the answer. It was basically the only thing Murphy ever purchased from the Triangle.

"Astute," Murphy Murphy deadpanned. He liked the kid, but not all that much.

"We just received a fresh supply so the refrigerator is full. I know because I filled it myself, manually by hand," Pravit smiled proudly and Murphy suddenly liked him even less.

"Good to know," he quipped and headed for the cooler. He pulled three cases, the most, thanks to experience, he knew he could manage to carry home. Murphy made his way back to the cash register and hoisted the cases on to the counter. Pravit scanned the barcodes.

"That will be one hundred and twenty-four dollars and twenty-four cents," he announced. Murphy Murphy reached into his back pocket for his wallet.

"Good news Mr. Double M squared," Pravit was beaming, "We are pleased to offer our very best customers a new opportunity." The young man had clearly practiced his pitch.

"And what might that be?" Murphy asked. He didn't really care.

"Well Mr. Double M squared,"

"That's too many M's," Murphy corrected in vain. Pravit continued unfazed.

"You see if you spend more than one hundred and twenty-five dollars on a single transaction, we are happily prepared to give you a free gift." He smiled proudly.

Murphy fumed because he was well aware that a gift, by definition, is free. But what disturbed him nearly as much was the fact that he'd have to spend an additional seventy-six cents for his "gift" so it was anything but "free".

"Just think," Pravit was sure he was setting the hook, "another seventy-six cents worth of merchandise would afford you this added bonus." He truly believed he had set the hook.

"For the love of God." Murphy Murphy couldn't contain his annoyance. He didn't want or need anything else and he was also pretty sure there wasn't anything in the store that cost only seventy-six cents. "Just the water, if you please." He counted out exactly one hundred and twenty four dollars and twenty-four cents.

"As you wish Mr. Double M squared." A clearly disappointed Pravit took the money and completed the transaction.

Back in the comfort of his home, Murphy settled into his favorite chair. A steaming mug of Darjeeling tea on the side table sat next to his mobile phone. Mozart's *Eine Kleine Nachtmusik: Allegro* seeped from his home stereo speakers. He had looked up Serious Crisis on the internet again and didn't enjoy the band's work anymore than he had the first time. He did, however, appreciate the art of music and held most musicians, even some rappers, in high esteem. He picked up the phone and punched in the numbers on the card Captain Hill had given him. After a handful of rings, the call went to voicemail.

"Hello. You've reached Jeffery Giucigiu, manager for New Beginning recording artists Serious Crisis. If you're inquiring about the band please leave a message. If this is personal, don't bother with a message. If I recognize the number, I'll hit you back." When he heard the beep, Murphy spoke.

"Mr. Giucigiu, my name is Detective Murphy Murphy and I am reaching out to you at the request of my superior officer Captain David Hill. He's led me to believe that he is related to one of the members of your troupe." Anticipating running out of his allotted message time he left a return number and disconnected. The tea was now at the perfect temperature and Mozart was on a roll. Murphy took a sip of one and then closed his eyes and drank in the other. He was hopeful his phone wouldn't ring for many minutes. Much to his chagrin his hopes were dashed.

"Murphy," the detective answered after turning down the music, setting down the mug, and picking up the phone.

"Is this the police gendarme Murphy?" a voice, Murphy correctly determined belonging to Jeff Giucigiu, asked.

"Is that supposed to be funny?" the detective had a question of his own.

"Maybe?" Giucigiu replied.

"Or maybe not," Murphy answered, then waited.

"Okay then," the manager decided to tread more lightly, "Is this Detective Murphy?"

"It is."

"This is Jeffery Giucigiu, from Serious Crisis"

"I know," Murphy Murphy interrupted.

"Returning your call," Giucigiu finished.

"Are you in a position to require my services?" Murphy got to the point.

"I'm not entirely sure," he started to answer.

"Well then I suggest that when you get to the point of being *entirely* sure, you give me a call then." Murphy started to hang up.

"Wait! Okay. Yes. I, uh we, need your help," the manager sputtered.

"With what?"

"Well, it appears possessions belonging to various members of the band have disappeared."

"It *appears* these possessions have disappeared or they *have* disappeared?" Murphy needed clarification.

"They have."

"How many?"

"Six so far."

"Band members or possessions," Murphy expanded his inquiry.

"Both," Giucigiu answered.

"And everyone has been affected?"

"That's correct."

"And you suspect all of the items, from each of the band members, have been stolen?"

"Seems the most logical explanation."

"Logical to whom?" Murphy Murphy wondered aloud.

"Well I guess to me, uh to us." Giucigiu answered. Murphy took a moment and the manager took advantage of the dead air. "We're headed your way for two shows. Can we meet in person?"

"Is there another way to meet?" Murphy asked, then added, "You have my number." He ended the call.

"What an ass." Giucigiu said into a disconnected line.

The tea was now too cold to drink, but Murphy turned up the Mozart believing, he had his first suspect.

Keith Hirshland

SOME TIME LATER IN TIME

Murphy Murphy stood in the shadows near a pillar that clearly held up part of the room. He had arrived at the venue hours before the show was scheduled to begin, wanting to get a better feel for what happens in the lead up before a rock 'n roll show. Murphy had gone back to the internet to get more information on his fair city's part in the band's tour and discovered Serious Crisis was scheduled for two shows in the 35,000-seat arena, which was home to both the city's main college and professional minor league basketball teams.

He reached out to Giucigiu to set up a meeting. During the course of that conversation the detective learned the band was slated to perform a third, more intimate show. It would be a private party and a favor to an old friend and financial backer who just happened to own one of the most popular rock and roll bars in the city.

Murphy Murphy was now a visitor in that particular venue, a room that could possibly hold one thousand souls, but only if the club's owner broke every rule in the fire inspector's book.

A young man entered the space carrying what looked to be a hose on his left shoulder. He headed to the corner of the room and dumped his load on the floor. It *was* a hose, but slightly more robust than the standard garden variety Murphy recognized from lawns all over the area. The person screwed one end into the hose bib on the wall and the detective detected that part of the cement floor was slightly higher than the spot at which Murphy Murphy stood. Upon further inspection he noticed the floor continued sloping past his position to an even lower point marked by a large drain covering. Murphy suddenly heard water running and turned to see the hose carrier had turned the knob on the bib and released the flow. A spray nozzle was now attached to the business end of the hose and with it the custodian started spraying the concrete floor. Water was flowing from high to low and into the drain.

That's an effective way to clean the floor of a rock 'n roll bar thought Murphy Murphy. Then he heard another, different noise. Glasses, or glass bottles, Murphy couldn't be sure, clinked behind him. He turned toward the sound and saw a woman setting a couple of bottles of alcohol on a bar that ran most of the length of the room's back wall. They looked like vodka bottles to Murphy. He walked away from one human in the room and toward the other.

"Hi," he said, hands in pockets, when he got near the bar. The woman, tall, pretty but once prettier, with a shock of bright purple in her dyed jet-black hair, looked up from the bottles.

"Help you?" she asked, then immediately went back to her task. Murphy Murphy watched. She unsealed a new, full, Russian branded vodka bottle. The detective didn't speak Russian but he surmised the words on the label translated to "premium rot gut" or "cheap crap good enough to get you drunk". He made a mental note to ask his friend Judith. He continued to observe as the woman behind the bar proceeded to pour the contents of the full bottle into the empty vessel by its side. Murphy knew the brand name of the bottle now being filled. It was because a famous actor told Murphy through his television screen that it was "the best tasting vodka in the world".

"Help you?" the woman repeated as the clear, supposedly odorless and tasteless, alcohol transferred from one bottle to the other.

"You here every night?" Murphy asked.

"Firstly, what possible business is that of yours? And secondly, how does any answer I give to that question help me get an answer *my* initial question?" She expertly replaced the cork stopper from the newly filled bottle with a standard bar pour spout and then reached underneath the bar for two more bottles.

"Detective Murphy Murphy," he said, pulling his shield from his coat pocket. She smiled a small, crooked smile. It made her still pretty features even prettier.

"You gonna arrest me for tapping the old well?"

"Ma'am, I have no interest in arresting you for anything, least of all doing whatever you're doing to the well," Murphy said politely. Her crooked smile became a laugh.

"Nice badge," she said

"Thank you," he replied

"How can I help you, officer?"

"Detective," he corrected

"How can I help you, detective?"

"I was doing some research," Murphy got straight to the point, "and learned the band Serious Crisis added a show, tonight," He swiveled his head to look around the room, "in here."

"I guess it was a sudden impulse." The bartender practically spat out her reply. Murphy Murphy suddenly thought she was a little less pretty.

"Aren't they all?" he asked

"All what?" she looked puzzled

"Impulses," he answered, "Sudden." Clearing it up for her.

"Now that you mention it…" She couldn't help but agree.

"You're welcome," he added

"You're cute," she said, changing the subject.

"Thank you," Murphy blushed. "Be that as it may, do you have any thoughts as to why Serious Crisis would play here? Tonight?"

"Goosh," was her one-word answer

"I beg your pardon?" Murphy looked confused because he was confused.

"Goosh," she repeated. "Jeff Giucigiu. The band's manager." She started the process of emptying and filling bottles again. "He and Gaston go way back. College, I think. Dartmouth."

"Gaston?" Murphy was trying to keep up

"Yeah. Gaston Carlucci. The guy that started this dump, err establishment. He made a boat load of money thanks to some insider trading stuff on Wall Street and decided to use it to sponsor a few rock bands. Thanks to Goosh, Serious Crisis was one of them." The detective waited to make sure she was finished.

"*Insider trading?*" He raised an eyebrow. She laughed out loud. *Pretty again*, thought Murphy Murphy.

"Just wanted to see if you were paying attention," she told him. "Gaston did come into a bunch of money and he did give some of it to Serious Crisis. But he came by it honestly. The band knows they owe Gaston. Since they hit the big time, they pay him back by performing here every once in a while for a thousand of Gaston's closest friends. As a favor."

"You seem to know quite a bit," Murphy praised the woman behind the bar.

"I better," she replied, "Gaston is my brother and this joint is half mine." She finished pouring and topped the second bottle with another pour spout. Then she wiped her right hand with a towel before extending it toward Murphy. "I'm Charlie. Charlie Carlucci." Murphy grabbed her hand and was surprised by both the softness of her skin and the strength of her grip. They shook. "Pleased to make your acquaintance, detective, I hope we can make this part of a regular routine." She smiled. Murphy, despite his reservations, smiled back.

He counted four rings as he waited for Judith Colman to pick up. On the fifth ring she did.

"Hey Murph." She sounded busy.

"Hi. Have you ever tapped the old well?" he asked.

"Excuse me?" Murphy noticed she didn't sound busy any longer. She sounded angry. "What business is that of yours?"

"I'm asking because while doing some legwork on a case I came across a woman behind a bar doing just that."

"What in the hell are you talking about?" Judith shot back.

"The woman. Behind the bar. She was pouring vodka from a full bottle of a clearly inferior brand into an empty bottle of an obviously more expensive one. I approached her, showed her my shield, and she asked if I was going to arrest her for "tapping an old well". Judith Colman laughed out loud. Murphy Murphy liked the sound of it. He had always enjoyed the sound of Judith's laughter.

"Oh Murphy," she replied post laughing fit. "Do you have any idea what "tapping an old well" means?"

"I assume it means the precise activity that I just described."

"And you couldn't be more wrong. I suggest you Bing the phrase and get back to me with your apology."

"*Bing* the phrase?" Once again Murphy was confused during a conversation.

"Yeah *Bing* it. Look it up, Google it," she clarified. "And for the record, I have never "tapped an old well" behind, in front, or on top of any bar." She hung up. He called back.

"What now?"

"Do you want to see Serious Crisis tonight?" he asked.

"Sounds fun but the show is not tonight, Murph. It's tomorrow night and a second one on Saturday. I have tickets for Saturday night's concert already."

"They're playing tonight too," Murphy corrected his friend. "It's a private show while they're in town. Nine o'clock at the Gas Pump Lounge."

"Gaston and Charlie's joint?"

"You know it? Them?"

"Sure. The Pump is a crazy good place to see a show."

"So, you wanna come with me?"

"I want to but I can't. I'm already taking Saturday night off. Practically had to offer the Pizzer something above and beyond the call of duty to get it. There's no way he'd let me outta here tonight too. Plus, I don't have anybody to watch the boys." Murphy knew she was talking about her dogs. He also knew he'd be going solo tonight. "But you have fun," she added.

"Ok. Will do. Oh, and maybe you should tell your friend Charlie Carlucci to stop 'tapping old wells'".

"Jesus, Murph," she said before hanging up. "Would you please quit saying that." And she was gone for good.

Murphy smiled and stuffed his phone into the front right pocket of his pants. He turned to go back into the bar through the same door from which he exited but found he couldn't. There was no handle, no doorknob. Nothing to pull or turn to gain entrance. No way to get back inside, at least not through that door, not without help from inside. He knocked and waited. After a half minute or so he hammered on the door a handful of times with the fat part of his fist. Nothing.

Murphy Murphy took stock of his surroundings. He couldn't recall having ever been in this exact place before. It was an alley, brick buildings on either side, just wide enough, he figured, for his mom's 1977 Cadillac Coupe de Ville to squeeze through, as long as nobody's arms were hanging outside an open window. He thought about the car his mother drove. Her Caddy was two-tone; yellow body, white top. He remembered how much she loved that car.

Murphy left memory lane and headed out of the alley and on to the street. He looked left then right and saw the main entrance to the club. Walking that way, he passed a 3' by 5' glass and metal case mounted on the outside of the brick. Through the dirty glass he could see a black sandwich board with white letters pressed into the grooves. He read the bigger letters at the top, "The Gas Pump Lounge", the name of the "dump" co-owned by his new bartender friend. Below the name, in smaller letters, were several rows of dates and artist's names. Last Friday night somebody named Pat Green had performed. Next week a band called Post Animal would headline. This particular day's date was there but the space where Serious Crisis should have been was filled by "Private event Invite only". *You need a comma* Murphy thought as he walked on.

The detective found the door through which he had entered when he first arrived and went through it again. Like before, he bounded down the ten or so steps and found himself in the same, slightly slanted floor space. He hadn't gone up any steps when he left the building to call Judith, so he had a look around to see if he could identify his exact exit, the door with no exterior handle. Before he could find it, his eyes lit on Charlie Carlucci. She was still behind the bar. Instead of transferring liquor from one bottle to another she was engaged in a conversation with two men seated in front of her. As Murphy continued to watch he realized she was more of an observer than an active participant in the tête-à-tête. Both of the men sat with their back toward Murphy, but he surmised one was Gaston Carlucci and the other was the reason he was here in the first place, Jeffery Giucigiu.

In A Completely Different Place at the Exact Same Time

Walter "DeMaio" Turrell was stretched out on the sofa in one of the band's two tour busses. The vehicles were parked, nose to tail, on a side street not far from The Gas Pump Lounge. Members of the road crew were busy unloading the necessary gear for that evening's show from the bays of the busses. Some golf tournament was playing on the satellite TV, but Turrell was neither watching nor listening. His ears were plugged by ear buds, his eyes were closed, and the fingers gripped what was left of a joint. He didn't hear the knock on the bus door, didn't open his eyes until he felt Lyndsay Howlund plop down on the sofa, near his feet.

"Stray dog," he said as a greeting after opening his right eye. He popped the earbuds out with one hand and offered her the joint with the other.

"You know that's not legal in this state," she said, declining. He accepted her refusal by taking a toke.

"Backwards bastards," he said in a strained voice, exhaling at the same time. "Flawed species," he added. Howlund chuckled. "What can I do for you Lynds?"

"You think we'll have to talk to the police?" She asked, picking at a cuticle.

"Haven't given it any thought," he answered immediately. "Maybe. Probably. I guess." He offered up the joint again and this time Lyndsay refused with a shake of her head. He pinched the ember out with the tips of the thumb and forefinger of his right hand. A wisp of smoke curled upward. "Why?"

"Just curious." She looked down at her shoes and then up at her band mate.

"Look, stuff's missing. Been stolen. Some of it, like my lighter, was expensive. The cops are going to need details, descriptions."

"Yeah, I know. But can't Jeff just give him the list? Tell him the what and the when?"

"What am I missing here?" Turrell studied his friend, "According to Goosh, you're the one who technically brought the police into this by telling your mom, who told your uncle, who just happens to be a cop."

"*Technically* yes," she answered. "But I was just talking to my mom. I wasn't sure she'd say anything to Uncle Dave. I didn't ask her to. But geez, somebody is taking stuff that belongs to us. *Violating* us and I want to find out who. I just didn't think this would happen so quickly." She laughed, slightly embarrassed.

"You hiding something stray dog?" he asked with a smile.

"Always." She smiled back.

"Look, it's no big deal. If we do have to talk to the po po just tell them what you know," he reassured her. "The best that can happen is we get our stuff back; the worst, we don't. Simple as that."

"Simple as that," she repeated. She put her hands on her knees and started to rise. "I'm gonna try and find a Chinese chicken salad. Want something?"

"No thanks," he said, opening a drawer and pulling out a container of double stuffed Oreo cookies, "But thanks." Lyndsay shook her head, touched her friend on the knee, and left.

Murphy Murphy watched Charlie Carlucci. Her consideration shifted between the two men at the bar, depending on which one was speaking. One of the men had long, past the shoulder, hair; the other had short hair, stylishly cut and graying around the temples. Charlie wiped the bar with a rag. Murphy could see she was attentive, especially when "long hair" spoke. *Must be her brother Gaston* Murphy thought. He wore faded blue jeans, a tee shirt that had seen better days and cowboy boots. Murphy could only see the back of the shirt, but he knew the front featured the image of a musical act because what he could read was dates and cities from a long-ago tour.

The other fellow, the one Murphy figured was Jeff Giucigiu sported a long-sleeved gingham shirt, navy blue and white, a pair of khakis and athletic shoes; *expensive ones* thought Murphy. He looked from the shoes back up to Charlie and found her gaze directly on him. Her lips formed a slight smile and for the second time that day Murphy felt flush. The two men must have realized they'd lost Charlie's attention because they turned at the same time to see what had become more interesting than them. Murphy Murphy held up his left hand in a wave-free wave. Neither man responded, but Charlie tilted her head slightly; a gesture Murphy took to mean, "come on over" and he did.

Charlie squirted water from a nozzle into a red plastic cup and set it on the bar just to the left of her brother.

"Detective Murphy," she said as a greeting.

"Detective," the man in the gingham shirt echoed.

"Detective?" Gaston Carlucci asked, looking first at Murphy, then at his sister.

"Miss Carlucci," Murphy nodded in the bartender's direction, grabbed the cup and took a long drink of the water. Putting it down, he addressed the other two. "Gentlemen, my name is Detective Murphy

Murphy and I'm fairly certain," he looked at Gaston, "you are Gaston Carlucci," then he looked at Jeffrey, "and you are Jeffery Giucigiu." He took another drink.

"Guilty as charged," Giucigiu said with a smile. "Get it? Guilty? Come on!" he pleaded to Charlie, "He's a detective! That was funny." Murphy could tell Charlie must not have agreed.

"Detective?" Gaston repeated his question. Murphy got a look at the front of his tee shirt and noticed the band on tour was Everything But The Girl. Murphy Murphy liked Everything But The Girl, so he decided he was going to like Gaston Carlucci.

"Mr. Carlucci. I am here at the invitation of your friend here, Mr. Giucigiu. I was fortunate to make the acquaintance of your sister a short time ago and now I am pleased to meet you." Gaston looked at Murphy, then at Charlie and finally at Giucigiu.

"A *Detective*?"

"Relax Gaston," Giucigui put his hand on Carlucci's shoulder in an effort to reassure him, "The detective is indeed my invited guest." At that, Murphy Murphy rolled his eyes, Charlie smiled, Gaston sat, mouth open, motionless, and Giucigiu continued, "But it's got nothing to do with you. It's band stuff."

Murphy could see that explanation, with or without the shoulder touch, didn't have the desired effect on

Gaston Carlucci and what Gaston said next confirmed it.

"It's been my past experience," he started. Murphy looked at Charlie and slowly mouthed, "Oh. My. God." As Gaston continued, "that when boys with badges show up in my bar, it ends up having something to do with me."

"Don't worry Gas," Charlie addressed her brother and this time Murphy noticed him relax a little, "I'll follow after the detective like a puppy dog," she looked at Murphy and winked, "and make sure his focus stays on Serious Crisis." With that, Gaston swiveled slightly in his barstool and extended his right hand.

"Detective Murphy Murphy was it?"

"It was and it remains," Murphy said as he grabbed Gaston's right hand with his own.

"I'm Gaston Carlucci and it's a pleasure to welcome you to The Gas Pump Lounge."

"The pleasure is all mine," Murphy replied and the two shook hands. The detective looked past Gaston to the other man seated at the bar. "Mr. Giucigiu, shall we talk about why I'm here?"

"Call me Jeff and give me a minute. I gotta see a man about a horse." Murphy had no idea what that meant and his look showed it. "I gotta work on my short game." Different phrase, same look from the detective.

"Good grief Murphy." It was Charlie. "The man has to use the restroom." Murphy looked at the bartender.

"Well then why didn't he say that?"

"He did," Charlie replied.

"Twice," Gaston added and Jeff Giucigiu headed toward the men's room.

Without Advance Notice, DeMaio Turrell Gets A Visitor

DeMaio Turrell snored softly and had been sleeping like a dead guy since the minute Lyndsay left the bus. He was still stretched out on the tour bus sofa. The earbud had dislodged from his left ear while the right one remained intact. The TV was still on the Golf Channel. Big Joe Lionns and Chucky Gruber had come and gone at different times but Turrell never knew it. At this very moment he had company once more. The trespasser stood over the sleeping singer making sure the big man was dead to the world. Convinced, the unwanted guest moved to the back of the bus. Moments later, having gotten what they came for, the uninvited visitor left the bus without a sound. DeMaio Turrell slept on.

"Drink?" Charlie set a cocktail napkin in front of Murphy. Gaston was gone.

"What time is it?"

"What difference does it make?"

"I guess it doesn't but I just realized I didn't get lunch." Charlie slid a dish of mixed nuts next to the napkin.

"Drink?" she asked again. Murphy Murphy grabbed a couple of almonds and a cashew, popped them in his mouth, chewed and swallowed.

"Yes please. Jameson, neat." Charlie turned and grabbed two glasses from the shelf. It was a move he had seen his friend Judith make a million times. Next, she reached for the bottle of Irish whiskey, before she stopped and looked at Murphy. He watched as she set the bottle back in its place then squatted to grab a different, unopened bottle of the golden liquid from beneath the bar. She unscrewed the bottle top. Murphy smiled.

"What?" she asked, knowing what.

"I appreciate you not tapping this particular old well."

Charlie poured two fingers of Jameson into each glass, then raised hers.

"Slainte," she toasted. Murphy Murphy grabbed his glass and clinked it against Charlie's.

"Fad saol agat," he said with a smile. They drank.

A few minutes, or was it an hour, later (Murphy realized he had lost track of time), the band's manager returned to the bar and reclaimed his seat.

"Detective," he said again.

"Mr. Giucigiu," Murphy acknowledged the greeting and at the same time noticed the faint smell of dead skunk.

"Call me Jeff," Jeff said again.

"Jeff."

"Thanks for agreeing to meet with me. I'd like to help you completely eliminate anyone in the band from suspicion." A snort came from behind the bar and both men turned in time to see Charlie cover her mouth in an attempt to conceal a smile. Murphy was nonplussed.

"Then I'll need to talk to the band," the detective said.

"Well sure, if you think that's necessary."

"I do," Murphy answered.

"It'll take a few minutes to round them all up," Giucigiu looked at his watch, "And we've got a show."

"One member at a time," Murphy interrupted

"Umm. Okay, I guess," the manager drummed his fingers on the bar. "But why? I mean, part of my job is to look out for my gang, you know, and I was hoping to avoid a direct confrontation." The tiny bit of Murphy's patience, the bit that was hanging on for dear life, finally let go and drifted past Charlie and out the vent above the bar.

"And *my job* is to find whoever is responsible for perpetrating this crime against your *gang*."

"Yeah. Right. Sure," Giucigiu nodded, "So who do you want to talk to first?"

"Anybody but you," was the detective's answer.

The Interview Process Starts to Begin

"Another Irish?" Murphy looked up from his note pad to see Charlie, a towel slung over her right shoulder. She had changed. The tee shirt replaced with a white button down. Her hair, before hanging down around her shoulders, was now pulled back into a tight ponytail. *She looks nice* Murphy thought.

"You look nice," Murphy told her, "and no thanks to the Irish. Got work to do," he added.

"Thank you, good sir," she replied and walked away. A few other people had come into the club. Whether they were early concert arrivers or early drinkers who just wandered in off the street, Murphy was unsure.

"You the cop?" the voice came from behind Murphy Murphy.

"Detective," Murphy replied without turning around. "Why don't you have a seat." It was a statement, not a question.

"Don't mind if I do," DeMaio Turrell pulled up the barstool next to Murphy's.

"You are?" Murphy asked, turning to face his first interview.

"DeMaio Turrell at your service," the lead singer answered before he turned his attention to Charlie. "Excuse me," he raised his hand getting her attention, "Could I trouble you for a beer?" She smiled and headed his way.

"Hey Walt," she said, "Which one?"

"Walt?" Murphy asked his guest. "Walt is not DeMaio," he added, jotting down something in his note pad.

"How about the Sierra Nevada Pale Ale," he said to Charlie, pointing to the tap. "Given name is Walter," he said to Murphy, "but I didn't like it so I gave myself a different one."

"Fair enough," said the detective. They both watched Charlie perform a perfect pour.

"A detective huh?" Turrell sounded impressed, "The cop shop must be taking this one seriously." He grabbed his glass and took a long drink. Foamed settled on his upper lip and he left it there. Murphy decided he liked this guy.

"Tends to happen when one of the victims is the favorite niece of the department's Captain.

"Fair enough," Turrell nodded and took another drink. This time he wiped his mouth with his forearm and extended his hand. "You got a name, detective?"

"I do indeed," Murphy shook the singer's hand, "It's Murphy Murphy." Turrell smiled.

"Like New York, New York," he smirked, "A city so nice they had to name it twice. Or so the song goes," the singer said.

"A Rodgers and Hart song," Murphy nodded, "'Manhattan', I believe."

"So, you run the robbery division?" Turrell changed the subject.

"In reality, I don't," Murphy responded, "I'm head of the Department of Redundancy Department."

"Redundancy?" The musician looked quizzically at the detective. "Is that kinda like jumbo shrimp?"

"It's actually nothing like that," Murphy answered, "That would be an oxymoron." Turrell took another drink from his beer and nodded.

"So, more like racecar," he said thinking he had it, "You know, a word that's spelled the same forward and backward."

"Wrong again my new friend," Murphy liked this game, "Racecar is a palindrome and Detective Leon Noel is in charge of that department. Redundancy is the superfluous repetition or overlapping, especially of words."

"What the heck?" Turrell stared at Murphy, "What did you do, memorize the dictionary?"

"Yes," Murphy said, not skipping a beat. "Some examples of redundancy would be 'foreign imports', or 'pair of twins', or 'round in shape', or," he paused half a beat and made sure Turrell was paying attention, 'serious crisis'". Turrell was indeed paying attention and gave the detective a warm, broad, smile. "Now why don't you tell me what was stolen from you and when." The singer nodded, ordered another beer, and did.

Murphy Murphy rested his forehead on the bar, his personal Moleskine notebook providing an inadequate pillow. His arms hung by his side. Half his rear end rested on the barstool, the other half did not.

"Having fun?" Charlie had approached.

"More than I can say." The detective had just spent, in his mind, too many minutes with Herbert Tolles Albanese, Charles no middle name Gruber, and Big Joe Lionns.

"What can I get you?" Charlie asked

"How about the last thirty minutes of my life back?" Murphy lifted his forehead off the pad.

"Can't help you there, but how about a Jameson? On the house."

"Tempting," Murphy admitted, "but I'm on the clock. Just water."

"You got it copper," she said, reaching for the dispenser.

"How many records has this band sold?" Murphy Murphy asked Charlie Carlucci a few minutes and another glass of water later. He had spoken to four members of Serious Crisis but had yet to spend any time at all with Captain Hill's niece, Lyndsay, or any meaningful minutes with the group's manager. The one guy about which Murphy still, deep down, harbored suspicions.

"I don't think they call them records anymore, Murphy," the detective was told for the second time that week. "But that's not where the money is these days."

"It's not?" he wondered aloud.

"Nope," she answered. "Ticket sales is a big part of it. Big tours with large, sold out arenas. But these days the real money is in commercials."

"Commercials?" Murphy was now completely confused.

"You bet," she said emphatically. "Corporations pay big bucks for songs to play in the background as they sell their products on TV."

"No kidding?"

"No kidding. And these guys have two on the air right now. One's a car commercial and the other's pushing feminine hygiene products. The actual fact is they're pretty catchy."

Murphy shook his head. "I don't want to know but they sure must be making a ton of dough."

"Why do you say that?" the bartender asked.

"The things that are missing? The stuff that's been stolen? It's crazy."

"Go on," Charlie leaned in.

"An eighteen hundred dollar lighter, a corkscrew that cost almost as much and a seven hundred dollar kangaroo whip, handmade by someone named Spanky, just to name a few."

"A seven hundred dollar *bullwhip*?" Charlie shook her head

"I don't believe I said bullwhip."

"Is there another kind?"

"I believe there are six distinct types of whips. The aforementioned bullwhip, the snake whip, the signal whip, the stock whip, the cow whip, and the Bullock whip."

"Kinky," she winked. He winked back. "Is that the sum total?" she asked, hoping to goad him into a reaction. He didn't bite.

"And did you know a bow tie can cost two hundred and fifty bucks!"

"Now *that's* outrageous!" Carlucci smiled, leaned across the bar and gave Murphy a quick kiss on the cheek. "Did I mention you're cute?" And she was gone. Murphy's cheeks reddened as his eyes followed her down the bar. He hadn't realized the place was beginning to fill up. He guessed the show would start fairly soon and that meant he had missed his chance to speak with either Lyndsay Howlund or Jeff Giucigiu.

He scanned the room. The crowd filing in and milling around appeared to be relatively young, at least by Murphy's definition, and pretty well off. Men in nice jeans or khakis, several wore sport coats. A fair number of women in dresses and what looked to be expensive shoes or boots. Murphy thought back to the custodian with the hose and hoped the footwear would survive the evening.

One straggler seemed completely out of place. Murphy Murphy homed in on him, a man standing near the edge of the stage, near some speakers. He was talking to another person, clearly someone associated with either the club or the band, who was setting guitars on stands. The man in question wore a Hawaiian shirt, a pretty old one, on top of a long sleeve white undershirt. Cargo shorts and athletic style knee socks added to the look. His feet were covered by Huarache style sandals. The kind with the thick tire tread soles. His hair was short in the front, quite long in the back and going gray. Murphy could also see glasses suspended around his neck with what looked like a shoestring. They were the type of reading glasses that separated in the middle.

"How did the interviews go?" Murphy's attention was interrupted by Jeff Giucigiu.

"Fine," he answered curtly. "Do you know that person standing near the edge of the stage?" Murphy didn't look at Giucigiu while the manager looked toward the stage.

"In the Hawaiian shirt?" he asked

"In the Hawaiian shirt."

"Oh, that's just Mags," the manager said in a matter of fact tone.

"*Just* Mags?" Murphy asked, "What's his real name?"

"No idea. Started coming to shows a while ago, now we see him everywhere. We all just know him as Mags. Guess you could call him a groupie. The band loves him."

"Do they now?" Murphy wondered aloud and pulled out his phone and took a couple of pictures. Then he made a note or two in his pad. *You never know* he thought.

Meanwhile the Band was Backstage Doing Some Advanced Planning

Chuckie Gruber tuned one of his guitars, Herbie Albanese twirled a drumstick between the fingers of his right hand, Big Joe sipped a glass of wine and Lyndsay Howlund stared into space. DeMaio Turrell noticed one of them.

"Penny for your thoughts stray dog," he said, sitting down next to Lyndsay.

"Oh, hey Walt," she acknowledged her company, "Just running some lyrics for a new song around in my brain." Turrell didn't buy it.

"Cool," he said anyway, "Give me a taste."

"Way too soon," she deflected, "Nothing concrete yet but I'm thinking the title is going to be 'Unintended Mistake'." That made Turrell think about his conversation with Murphy Murphy just a few hours before.

"Sounds perfect," he said and Lyndsay smiled a sad smile.

"So, what did everybody tell the police officer?" It was Lionns who swirled the red wine around and put the glass up to his nose.

"You mean detective," corrected Herbie.

"Officer, detective, what's the difference?" Joe asked.

"You mean besides experience, smarts and a couple of pay grades?" interjected Gruber.

"That's a true fact," exclaimed Herbie, pointing his drumstick in the guitarist's direction.

"Whatever," dismissed Lionns, "So, what did everyone tell him?" he repeated, asking his original question.

"I told him I wanted my darn whip back," Herbie shouted.

"I bet that was helpful to the investigation," Big Joe smirked.

"I haven't spoken to him yet," Lyndsay added.

"What did he ask you?" Turrell had wandered over to Chuckie with a bottle of beer in each hand. He gave one to his buddy.

"Thanks," Gruber grabbed the beer and twisted off the cap. He took a drink. "He just asked a bunch of questions about my corkscrew. You know, where I bought it? How much did it cost? How long I had it?

Where and when do I remember seeing it last?" He took another pull from the beer. "He also asked if I remembered who I was with the last time I saw it and if I had any idea who might want the thing more than me."

"Do you?"

"Do I what?"

"Have any idea who might want a fancy corkscrew more than you?"

Gruber thought for a second. "To tell you the truth DeMaio that could be a long list."

"What do you mean?

"Well, it's just. I mean. Look, I had kinda lost interest in the thing. Hadn't even used it in months." He looked up at his friend. "Drinking wine alone is a pain in the butt," he smiled. Turrell smiled back.

"This wine is really good Chuckie!" Lionns shouted out, almost on cue. "What is it?"

"It's an Oregon Pinot Noir Joe," Gruber answered before he turned back to Turrell. "Willamette Valley, Domaine Serene 'Monogram'," he clarified. "Three hundred bucks a bottle," he clarified further.

"Jesus! And you're letting Big Joe guzzle it?"

"Sure, why not?" he shrugged. "Silly me, I thought I was being cool buying two, three, and four hundred-dollar bottles of wine. Actually, it *did* pay off on a couple of occasions with a few babes." Turrell tipped his beer bottle toward Gruber's in salute to his best friend. "But you know me Walt," Gruber touched his bottle to Turrell's. "We've been friends for years, heck I'd say best friends. We started this band together, started a few bands together."

"Some of them were big time," Turrell said softly. Remembering.

"I got no business buying a bottle of Screaming Eagle Napa Valley cabernet and even less business storing it in a motel mini fridge or on our tour bus. And I also got tired of hearing my financial guy bitch at me."

"Touché Charles," Turrell used his friend's given name. "So, who do you think took the corkscrew?"

"No idea."

There was a knock on the dressing room door. "Fifteen minutes folks," came the call from the other side.

"Thanks," Turrell called back. "Ok who's got the set list?" he asked the room.

"Right here," Herbie held up a sheet of paper. "We're opening with 'Commute Back and Forth'."

"Gawd I hate that song." It was Lionns again

"Why so Grumpy Big Joe? Turrell said walking past his friend toward the bathroom.

"Not grumpy. I just hate that song."

"But you wrote it," Gruber said with a laugh.

"Exactly," said Joe, finishing the remaining wine in one gulp.

"Excuse me, Mr. Mags is it?" Murphy had approached the man in the Hawaiian shirt and was now standing by his side. Mags smelled of cigarettes and cologne. *Polo* thought the detective.

"No Mr., mister," Mags answered without looking at Murphy, "Just Mags."

"Ok for now," the detective replied. "So, what are you doing here *just* Mags?"

"You writing a book?" was the response.

"Maybe."

"Then leave the 'just Mags' chapter out."

Murphy Murphy smiled and took the moment to get a closer look at Mags. The shirt was authentic Hawaiian and Murphy had seen dozens of them during his last trip to the islands. He even bought a couple that were now hanging in the back of one of his closets at home. The one hanging on Mags was well worn, but clean. The undershirt was similar to ones worn by professional athletes. His cargo shorts were relatively new and Murphy couldn't help but observe that several of the pockets were full. He noticed at least two mobile phone-like devices. The Huaraches, like the shirt, had seen their share of miles but the socks looked like Mags had just pulled them from a six-pack you buy at a department store. It was an interesting dichotomy in Murphy's opinion, a combination of comfort and costume.

"One more time," Murphy again addressed the man, this time placing his shield in Mags's peripheral vision, "What are you doing here?"

"And one more time," he took the time to glance at the badge, "*dee tec tive*, it's none of your business. This dog doesn't rollover, Rover. Now if you'll excuse me, I'm absolutely certain my favorite band is about to take the stage."

"I'll find you later then, *just* Mags. You can count on that."

"Knock yourself out detective," he said, starting a rhythmic clapping. The crowd around them noticed and joined in while Murphy Murphy made his way back to the bar thinking Jeffery Giucigiu wasn't the only person worth a closer look.

A few minutes later Serious Crisis did take the stage. Albanese took his seat behind the drum set and immediately started beating the big kick drum. Howlund, Gruber, and Turrell sauntered onto the platform together, the latter two giving a right-hand wave to the audience. Lyndsay, head down, made a beeline to a keyboard and started plunking out a couple of notes. Two guitars were behind her. For reasons Murphy didn't know, Big Joe was last and he walked the length of the stage like he owned it.

"Big Joe!" some in the crowd yelled.

"Roar Lionns Roar!" screamed others.

Maybe he did own it thought Murphy. As he looked at the stage, from his left to right, he saw Chuckie Gruber, then Turrell, then Lyndsay Howlund, and Big Joe Lionns. Herbie Albanese was behind them on a riser. That's what he saw. What he heard was a cacophony. Chords from a keyboard and guitars, single bass notes, and a myriad of voices saying, "test, test," or "check, check, one, two" into microphones. All the while the thump, thump, thump, courtesy of Herbie's right foot, kept time. There was an energy coming from the stage. The crowd could sense it and they whooped and hollered. Murphy felt it as well.

"Well, hello again Gas Pump Lounge!" It was Turrell. "Before we start, we want to thank Gaston and Charlie for giving us safe haven from the rock 'n roll storm." He looked toward the bar and the crowd cheered. "But most of all we want to thank you all for taking the time to come hear us play." The audience roared in approval again.

"I LOVE YOU LYNDSAY!" someone shouted. Murphy saw her smile. It was a million dollar smile.

"Well you can't have her chum," Turrell shot back, "because we love her too!" Everybody laughed. "Seriously folks, thanks a bunch for coming. We can't ever adequately express how much your support means." Murphy was impressed.

"Just play!" cried another voice, clearly not as impressed as Murphy, from the back of the room.

"Oh, don't you worry," Turrell assured, "We're gonna play. We see some old friends."

"Hi Mags!" Herbie interrupted from his perch

"And some new friends." Turrell continued. Murphy was sure the lead singer was looking his way. "And as far as each individual person is concerned, I hope you like the show." Then he winked. Right at Murphy Murphy.

"1, 2, a 1, 2, 3…" Herbie counted them in and the room filled with Serious Crisis.

Several songs in, Murphy, despite his preference for Mozart, found himself enjoying the show. He even recognized one of the songs. The one from the car commercial.

"What do you think?" It was Charlie.

"I think you're making money hand over fist pouring people rotgut and charging them for Grey Goose."

"About the band," she said, ignoring the jab.

"They're actually quite good. Both DeMaio and Lyndsay can really sing."

"Hey Mo Mo." It was Howlund. "Can I get a little more DeMaio and a lot less Herbie in my ear, please."

"While you're at it," Big Joe piped in. "I'd like just the opposite. Thanks Mo Mo."

"Who are they talking to?" Murphy asked Charlie

"Morris Morrison, their sound engineer. The guy that turns noise into music. Just ask him."

"Mo Mo," Murphy said

"Mo Mo," Charlie repeated.

"Is he at every show?"

"I would imagine. He's their guy. I think he also drives the tour bus."

"Mo Mo," Murphy said to himself. One more person he needed to talk to.

"This next song," Turrell again, "was our first 100,000 download." The crowd went crazy again clearly knowing what was coming next. "It's from our second CD, *Basic Fundamentals* and it's called, 'Future So Bright'." With that introduction Lyndsay, Chuckie and Big Joe all grabbed black shades and put them on. Some in the crowd pulled glasses of their own from pockets and purses and did the same. They continued to scream as Herbie put sunglasses on his face and started his count. Suddenly DeMaio Turrell threw up his right hand and Herbie stopped.

"Where are my Latch Alphas?" Turrell said off mic but loud enough for everyone in the club to hear. "They're always right here on my amp!"

Murphy figured "Latch Alphas" were DeMaio Turrell's sunglasses. Emphasis on "they were" because they appeared to be missing. So was Mags. The detective looked stage right and stage left but couldn't see a Hawaiian shirt anywhere in the crowd. He slid off his stool and headed for the first exit he saw. Outside he looked first left, then right. There were several people out, strolling up and down the street, enjoying the evening but as far as Murphy Murphy could tell none of them were "just Mags".

Keith Hirshland

For a Period of Hours Murphy Murphy Struggled to Get to Sleep

Murphy tossed and turned. For the dozenth time he looked at the clock on his bedside table. At the moment it was eleven minutes later than the last time he looked. Exasperated, he rolled out of bed, slipped into his house shoes, and padded into the kitchen. He hoped a cup of tea and a taste of Mozart might help.

Murphy ran the events of the afternoon and evening through his mind. Again. The interviews, the initial run in with the mysterious Mags, the show, the commotion around the missing sunglasses, the disappearance of the aforementioned Mags, and Charlie Carlucci. The alluring Charlie Carlucci. He scrolled through a playlist on his phone and happily settled on *The Concerto for Piano and Orchestra Number 23 in A Major*. With a press of a finger music filled the room and Murphy settled into his favorite chair to think.

"Who's Mags? Why did he leave so abruptly and where did he go?"

"How, if at all, is the sound engineer Mo Mo and the band's manager Jeff Giucigiu involved?"

"Is there a commonality to the missing items? A reason the thief selected them? Is one person, or more than one person, responsible?"

Mozart played on.

"Was Charlie Carlucci flirting with him or was she just a friendly person?" Murphy asked the questions one by one, out loud. As he closed his eyes, sleep came. He drifted off thinking of Charlie's lips on his cheek.

The tea kettle was whining. Murphy opened his eyes and took a peek at his phone. He had dozed off and missed seventeen minutes of Mozart and wasted a kettle full of Mountain Valley Spring Water. He awakened with a revelation. He pressed another icon on his phone and tapped out the internet address for an online buying and selling site. There was a rectangular bar at the top of the page inviting him to "Search for Anything". Murphy did. First, he typed Carne d'Ache lighters and pressed the little magnifying glass. More than two dozen options appeared, with two of the lighters on sale for $2,500 each, but none matched the one described by DeMaio Turrell. He went through the same process and searched for corkscrews, and then whips, with similar, unsatisfactory results. He set the phone down realizing the last thing any self-respecting crook would do is put his ill-gotten gains on a popular web site for all the world's law enforcement officers to see. The last few notes of Mozart played, Murphy rose, turned off the heat on the stove without ever pouring a cup of tea, and went back to bed.

Hours later a ringing phone jarred him from his slumber. The phone was his, the caller was his Captain, Dud Hill.

"Hullo," Murphy croaked out.

"Detective Murphy, I need to see you."

"Yes Sir."

"And I need that to happen before the clock on my wall hits twelve noon." He hung up. Murphy realized it was ten minutes after ten.

"It's just noon!" he yelled at the phone. "You know the twelve is redundant, don't you?" he added to no one and everyone.

Another Day Completely Filled with Surprises

"Have you made any positive progress on the case?" The clock on Captain Hill's wall said 11:57.

As opposed to negative progress? Murphy thought, standing at attention. "It's only been a couple of days," he said.

"Umm hmm," the Captain rubbed his temples with the middle fingers of each hand. "I think you know by now it's not my usual custom…"

My gosh will it EVER end? Murphy wondered

"To handcuff my detectives, especially this early in an investigation, but I've got some bad news."

"What might that be?" Murphy asked.

"Did you attend the private performance by Serious Crisis last night?"

"I did."

"Did you harass any patrons?"

"I did not!" Murphy was adamant in his defense.

"Well this office has received a complaint."

"From who? For what?" Murphy got was getting angry.

"Don't get defensive, detective," the Captain shook his finger at Murphy. "A patron called anonymously to complain that he had been harassed by one of this department's detectives. All I'm asking is whether or not that detective might have been you, Detective Murphy. I'd like you to reflect back."

"Might have been but it wasn't," Murphy answered, not the least bit defensively. "I spoke to a few people and asked a number of questions."

"Well this person saw it different and is threatening legal action." Murphy slowly shook his head. *Just Mags* he thought, *who, or what, is this guy?*

"So, let me spell this out in detail," the Captain finished, "If it *was* you, I strongly suggest you back off. Capice?" The detective looked at his Captain. Trying to decide if he was more disturbed by the dressing down or the assault on the English language.

"Understood," was his reply. Murphy Murphy turned on his heel and left the office. With his head held high he headed toward his own office in the basement. As he passed through the cop shop, he was well aware of the eyes following his progress. He knew most of his colleagues had little, or no, respect for him and many talked about him behind his back. They thought his one-man department was insignificant, a joke even. He didn't care. What he

93

knew that they didn't was his insignificant, one man joke of a department came with advantages. Specifically, updated software and entry, with a secure password, to law enforcement databases that only department heads were privy to. The kind of information that was accessible through the brand-new computer on his desk. That's where he was headed now.

Murphy scrolled through the pictures he had taken of Mags at The Gas Pump Lounge, selected the one he determined was most revealing, and uploaded it into the National Crime Information Center database. Then he waited. Real life wasn't a popular TV show, so Murphy knew the search might take a while. He got up to make the cup of tea he didn't enjoy the night before. Leaning against his desk he sipped his drink and thought about calling Charlie, wondering about the possibility of seeing her again. He hoped she might be thinking the same. It took a little more than an hour but Murphy learned his subject had never committed a crime, at least according to NCIC. He was disappointed but, for reasons he couldn't quite put a finger on, he wasn't surprised. He decided to go get a bite to eat at Bar Flight even though the food there was, by most standards, inedible.

Buck was nowhere to be found when Murphy entered Bar Flight. That wasn't unusual because on this afternoon, like almost every afternoon, his presence was unnecessary. People did come for an afternoon pick me up, or to drown their sorrows, or to bask in Judith's company, but rarely in groups and almost never in the mood to start trouble. On those occasions Judith, the Pizzer, or whomever was tending bar had both a Louisville Slugger and a 12-gauge shotgun at the ready.

The bar was dark but Murphy could easily make out Faye and Randy, Bar Flight regulars, sitting at their usual corner table. He could also see a handful of the guys and girls from Fire Engine Company 5 at a high top. Two of the pub's six televisions were on; the 1983 movie *Eddie and the Cruisers* was playing on both. It was one of several movies Richie and, Murphy suspected, Judith kept next to an old DVD player behind the bar. The others were *Rocky*, *Raging Bull*, *Out of Sight* starring George Clooney and Jennifer Lopez, *The Princess Bride*, and *The Lion King*. In spite of the impressive library, it felt to Murphy like *Eddie and the Cruisers* was playing in the bar an awful lot. Michael Pare, or more specifically John Cafferty and the Beaver Brown Band belted out "On the Dark Side". The joint was actually a good spot to watch a game, or a golf tournament or, for obvious reasons, a prize fight. The detective greeted the firefighters with a wave of his right hand. He ignored the couple. Murphy was happy to see Judith working the bar and told her as much when he sat down.

"Good to see you too, Murph," she said, wiping the area in front of him.

"What are today's odds that Lou won't ruin a patty melt?" he had asked this question before.

"I'd say 60-40 in your favor," she smiled, giving him a fairly uncommon reply.

"Sounds too good to pass up."

"Wash it down with a glass of Gail's peach iced tea?" she offered.

"Is there any other way?" he accepted.

Lou and Gail had worked in the craft services industry for decades, making meals and snacks for people in the television and movie making business. The work was hard, but steady, until one day a hot shot son of a star wannabe producer had a bad reaction to a combination of designer drugs he was taking and blamed Lou's "famous" breakfast burrito. He ranted and raved and barfed and actually said the words, "You'll never work in this town again!' And Lou didn't, despite the fact that the kid was the only person on the crew that day who got sick. So the cook drove his food truck east, Gail faithfully by his side. They stopped in cities and towns along the way before finally ending up in Richie Pizzoni's kitchen making food that few people ordered and even fewer enjoyed. Gail's peach tea, on the other hand, was to die for.

"Gimme a sec to put your order in," Judith said while walking away. Murphy watched Namath get up and follow her to the kitchen.

"Not sure that meets Department of Public Health guidelines," he said to the dog's wagging tail. Then Murphy pulled out his note pad and refreshed his memory about the case of Serious Crisis.

"How was the show?" Judith was back. She set a knife and fork, rolled in a napkin, on the bar.

"I have to admit I enjoyed the music more than I thought I would," Murphy said, looking up from, then closing, his note pad.

"Excellent," she laughed, helping herself to a sip of Murphy's tea.

"It's an interesting case. Every member of the band, including the manager, has had something personal, and in many cases rather expensive, go missing during the last few months." Murphy forgot he had told Judith all of this already. Like the good friend she was, she listened like she was hearing it all for the first time.

"Any early leads?"

"Maybe. I don't have a great feeling about the manager."

"You're 'Spidey senses' tingling?" she interrupted

"My what?"

"Never mind Murph, go on."

"And I haven't been able to meet or speak with the band's traveling sound engineer. Someone named Mo Mo."

"Morris Morrisey?" Judith asked. Murphy consulted his notes.

"One and the same. You know him?"

"Not personally," she stole another sip, "but I sure know of him. You should too."

"And why, pray tell, is that?"

"Morris Morrisey, Mo Mo, is a jazz legend. Multiple Grammy awards, worked with the greats including Miles Davis, Brubeck, and The Monk. I own several of his CD's."

"Impressive," Murphy nodded his appreciation, "And now he's the sound engineer for a rock band full of kids. I, for one, find that odd."

"Odd or normal, he's not your guy detective," she said grabbing a plate from a well-built woman in her mid-60s.

"Hey Gail," Murphy said

"Hello detective Murphy," she replied and turned away.

"And why is this famous Mo Mo not my guy?" Murphy turned his attention back to Judith.

"First, he's got to be at least seventy years old by now and B," she smiled because she knew mixing up sequencing was another one of Murphy's pet peeves. He confirmed that with a stern look. "he's blind as a bat," she continued. "Been that way since a couple of bad cops beat the crap out of him in LA during the '92 riots."

Murphy was speechless, so he took a bite out of his patty melt. The look on his face told Judith she was overly optimistic about the whole 60-40 thing. She shrugged. He swallowed.

"Funny, Charlie said she thought he drove the tour bus in addition to his engineering duties."

"That would be an America's Got Talent level trick," she laughed at her own joke. "He's good, but not that good. Charlie?" she added

"So, cross one Morris Morrisey, aka Mo Mo off the suspect list," Murphy said ignoring her last one word question.

"Yes," Judith didn't persist, "Check Mo Mo off the list."

"There is another possibility," Murphy took another, smaller bite of the sandwich.

"I'm all ears."

"There's this fan, actually the manager described him as a groupie. Said the band loves him."

"Go on."

"Apparently, he just showed up one night, started coming to concerts and now hardly ever misses one. No matter where they play."

"Interesting," she prodded.

"Older guy," Murphy pictured Mags in his mind, "Kinda funny."

"Funny strange or funny ha ha?" Judith reached across the bar and grabbed the other half of Murphy's patty melt and took a bite. After one chew she spat it out. "Don't eat that!" she instructed Namath the dog, not Murphy.

"Definitely funny strange." Lost in thought he took another bite, half chewed and swallowed. "He had mostly gray hair, short in front, long in the back."

"Like a mullet?"

"Not exactly, but not exactly not. He was wearing an old Hawaiian shirt over a long sleeve t-shirt, newish cargo shorts and Mexican style sandals with knee high white athletic socks."

"Sounds to me like he just wanted to blend in."

"Oh!" Murphy suddenly felt like he had remembered the most important part, "He had at least two mobile devices in his pockets."

"Like cell phones?" she asked. "That doesn't sound out of place at all."

"That's just it," Murphy nodded, "Guy looked like he was playing a part. Left the show early and disappeared into the night before I could question him further." Murphy looked at his plate. "Didn't this used to come with fries?"

"Does our groupie have a name?"

"Nickname. Mags."

"Just Mags?"

"Exactly. I ran his photograph through the known criminals' database and came up empty." Murphy decided not to mention the part about the pending threat of litigation. Judith drank more tea.

"What if he's not a criminal?" she asked, setting the plastic cup on the bar.

"Or he just hasn't been apprehended."

"I love it when you speak cop." She punched him lightly on the arm. "But seriously, what if he is the polar opposite of a criminal?"

"You think he could be a cop?"

"Not out of the question."

"I hadn't considered that." Murphy polished off the last of the peach tea. "But I will now."

"Afternoon Mr. Double M squared!" Pravit was thrilled to see his detective friend in the convenience store again so soon.

"Not today Pravit," Murphy was less than thrilled to see the young man. "I just need a roll of antacids." He knew from experience that Lou's cooking could have ill-timed effects.

"We have a great deal on a six pack of Tummy Tums! Normally they are two dollars apiece but today, and only today Mr. Double M squared, you can get the six pack for twelve dollars and fifty cents," he said, beaming.

"That's too many M's, Pravit," he shook his head, "And that NOT a deal! Just give me a pack of Rolaids. Please," he added. He paid for the relief and headed back to the precinct.

At his desk Murphy retrieved Mags's picture from his phone for the second time that day. This time he uploaded it into a different law enforcement database. There was no time to make a cup of tea this go around as Murphy got a hit in minutes.

"Johnny 'Jack' Maginnes." Murphy stared at the screen. He recognized the face, but the mug shot front and center on his computer showed a younger fella. Short hair, cropped military style. "Navy Seal, Honorable discharge, awarded the prestigious Navy Star for valor in combat." As Murphy Murphy read the resume aloud, he became more and more impressed. "A cop for decades, Dallas PD, now a private investigator." He leaned back in his chair, "What in the world is going on?" He got up and made himself a cup of tea after all.

Back at his computer, Murphy scrolled the screen down. There was a second picture of Mr. Maginnes. This one showed the man from waist up, arms folded across his chest revealing a tattoo on each arm. The one he could see best was an angry looking seal, knife in its mouth, white sailor's cap on its head. "That explains the long sleeve t-shirt," Murphy said to no one in particular. He clicked on the icon to print out what he felt was relevant information, including the pictures, and shut down his computer.

"Hello, you've reached Jeffery Giucigiu, manager for New Beginning recording artists," Murphy recognized the message and waited for the beep.

"This is detective Murphy Murphy, Mister Giucigiu, and I guess you could say this is personal. I expect a return call at your earliest convenience." Murphy hit the red button on his phone. Ten seconds later, it rang.

"Detective, it's Jeff Giucigiu. Sorry I just missed your call." It seemed to Murphy that the manager was less than sincere. "What can I do for you?"

"Did you call my precinct and lodge a complaint against me?" Murphy hadn't planned to ask that question first but he decided no time like the present.

"I beg your pardon? A complaint? I have no idea what you're talking about. Why would I do such a thing? You're trying to help us." This time he sounded much more sincere.

"I still have a couple more interviews to conduct, including yours." Murphy pressed on. "When can we make that happen?"

"Whenever you say," Giucigiu acquiesced. "Today's a night off so I'm not sure where everyone is, but tomorrow is a show so the band should all be in one place."

"Tomorrow it is," Murphy decided, "Shall we say ten AM?

"Ouch," the manager reacted, "I did say tonight was a night off, didn't I? Better make it after noon."

"One o'clock then. And I'll expect some time with you, Miss Howlund and the elusive Just Mags."

"Mags? Why?"

"That's my concern."

"Understood. But when I said he was a 'groupie' I didn't mean he was part of the group. He's just a fan. He comes to shows."

"According to you he comes to a lot of shows."

"So he's loyal. His money's green."

"I'm sure he is and I'm certain it is," Murphy thought the conversation might be over. It wasn't.

"I have no way to get in touch with him," Jeff offered in excuse. When Murphy didn't react right away, he pressed on, "Although he does come to a lot of sound checks."

"And what time would that be?"

"Tomorrow? Let's see, the show is at eight so I'd guess five-ish."

"Then I will see you at one, Miss Howlund shortly thereafter, and Mags at five *ish*. Enjoy the rest of your day, Mr. Giucigiu." Murphy hung up before the manager could respond. He suddenly found himself with the rest of *his* day so he decided to see what Charlie Carlucci was up to.

Murphy Murphy Drops by The Gas Pump Lounge to See His New Personal Friend and The Result Is A Date

"Tea?" Charlie asked as they sat down, "I thought you were Irish, not British."

"Actually, I'm neither," Murphy answered. "I just like tea."

In reality he didn't like pretentious chain coffee store tea but he realized he really liked Charlie Carlucci. When she suggested they spend whatever time they had at the coffee shop around the corner from the bar, Murphy said sure. Having a cup of coffee, or tea, was a minimal commitment. If either person was looking to escape, it was an easy out.

"Did you order a doppio macchiato because of your Italian heritage?" He turned the question on her.

"Touché my new cute friend. Touché." It was the third time, Murphy recalled, that she had called him cute in less than twenty four hours. "What's going on with the case? Any news?"

Personally, Murphy felt the urge to tell her everything, but professionally he had reservations. He had already confided details of the case with Judith Colman because he knew he could trust her. He wasn't as sure about Charlie. He decided to tread lightly.

"Too early to say," he lied a little, "Still doing the legwork."

"No suspects? No late-night stakeouts during which you're looking for some company?" She winked at Murphy.

"You watch too much TV." He smiled, thinking about Charlie keeping him company.

"When you bolted out of the club last night it looked like you were onto something or someone."

"Sorry I left so abruptly."

"You don't have to apologize for leaving," she said, "But the jury is still out about you having to apologize for not coming back." She took a sip from her tiny coffee cup. Murphy had no retort. "Were you after the dude in the Hawaiian shirt?"

Murphy blew on his tea without taking a sip. He had yet to drink a drop of what the college aged barista called "Emperor's crown green tea". "What do you mean?"

Charlie set her tiny cup on the tiny saucer. "Come on flatfoot. If you and I are going to be friends you're going to have to open up. Don't you trust me?" She reached across the table and put her right hand on Murphy's left.

"A 'flatfoot' is a beat cop," he managed a reply. "I'm a detective." He turned her hand over in his and held it, fingers interlocked. They fit perfectly. "Ok," he said when she didn't pull back. "According to Jeff Giucigiu the *dude* in the Hawaiian shirt is a groupie. Just started coming to shows a few months ago."

"Well he certainly didn't look like the rest of the invitation only crowd last night. He stuck out like a sore thumb."

"I approached him during the soundcheck and he was reluctant, to say the least, to answer questions."

"Cops can be intimidating."

"No doubt," he agreed, "But this guy was anything but intimidated. I'd describe him as recalcitrant." Charlie looked at him quizzically. "Insubordinate," he offered, "Defiant."

"Thanks," she said quietly and squeezed his hand. "I'm guessing that's a red flag for a flatfoot," she smiled. He liked it.

"So, when all the commotion began—"

"The sunglass thing?" she interrupted.

"The sunglass thing," he confirmed, "And he bolted, which struck me as odd so I went after him."

"What was his excuse?" she asked. "For leaving?"

"No clue," was Murphy's answer, "Couldn't find him."

"And you didn't come back."

"And I didn't come back."

She finished her coffee. "So, what now?" she asked

"Now I have to wait until tomorrow. The band has a show at the arena and I've arranged to talk to the manager and then Lyndsay Howlund at one o'clock."

"And what about 'Chin Ho'?

"Who?" he asked.

"Chin Ho, you know, from Hawaii Five O? You're the one who told me I watched too much TV." Murphy looked at her like she was speaking Swahili. "Good grief Murphy. The guy in the Hawaiian shirt. What about him?"

"Mags. He goes by Mags."

"Of course he does." She shook her head.

"Jeff said soundcheck is at five. If history means anything, he'll be there." A comfortable silence settled between them as they continued to hold hands. Then Murphy thought of something. "Hey, did you know Morris Morrisey was blind?"

"Mo Mo? Of course. Everybody knows that."

Not everybody thought Murphy. "But you said you thought he also drove the tour bus."

"I was yanking your chain, silly. Thought you knew that."

"Do you want to go to the show with me?" Murphy changed the subject

"Now that's a heck of an offer," she deadpanned "but I have to work. Besides, one go 'round with Serious Crisis a week is enough for me. They're not exactly my cup of tea," she said, looking at Murphy's cup of tea. "But I *will* let you buy me dinner tonight."

"Deal," Murphy agreed, making a mental note to find out just what was Charlie Carlucci's musical cup of tea.

It didn't take very long for Murphy Murphy to discover Charlie's taste in music. It was Country. After a delightful dinner she suggested they have an after-dinner drink at a place called Buckaroo Bonzai's. Murphy thought it sounded interesting and readily agreed. Turned out the joint was a cowboy/sushi bar complete with spicy tuna hand rolls and a mechanical bull, all in the same room.

The place was huge and it was packed. Murphy wasn't surprised he had never been there before but he was taken aback that he'd never even heard of it. Charlie on the other hand was clearly a regular. Both the bouncer and the bartender greeted her by name and her "go to" drink. A shot of Tattoo tequila and a bottle of beer suddenly appeared on the bar.

"Who's your friend?" the bartender had asked.

"This is Murphy," she'd answered.

"Had a dog named Murphy once," he showed his smile beneath a Sam Elliott mustache. "Big dog. Newfoundland."

"Kinda goes without saying," Murphy half-smiled back.

"Be nice." It was Charlie. Murphy was uncertain at which of the men the admonishment was directed. Both, he'd figured.

"Please to make you acquaintance, Murphy," Sam Elliot mustache offered a calloused hand to shake. "What'll it be?"

"Pleasure's mine." Murphy shook. "I'll have what she's having."

What he and Charlie ended up also having was a great time. The evening included another shot of tequila and a trip or two around the dance floor. Somehow Murphy knew Charlie would be an excellent dancer but she seemed astonished to learn Murphy was no slouch. He walked her home and asked if he could kiss her goodnight. She suggested one last nightcap inside, but he declined and they kissed. She commented on what a gentleman he was and thanked him for a wonderful evening with a perfectly executed curtsy and another, longer kiss. He remembered his whole body tingling as he stepped back and offered a bow.

"Til next time, milady," he said and stole one last kiss on the lips before heading home. It felt to Murphy Murphy like his feet never touched the ground. Later, in his bed, he replayed more of the evening. They had learned a little more about each other. Charlie confessed to being married once, for almost six years, about twelve years ago. Murphy confided that, in his professional experience, ex-husbands could sometimes be problematic.

"Not this one," Charlie said with certainty. When Murphy asked how she could be so sure, she explained her ex had left her for his hairdresser, moved to Costa Rica and bought a fishing boat. Murphy said something about how stupid both decisions were and she smile and said, "It gets better." It did. It seems the ex-went out fishing one night, alone, and never came back. The Costa Rican authorities found the boat days later adrift at sea with no sign of human life. They chalked it up to a tragic accident and since no one had bothered to change the beneficiaries on his three-million-dollar life insurance policy, Charlie received a very large check in the mail.

"I invested some," she told him while downing a shot of tequila, "and I used the rest to buy my share of The Pump," she told him, referring to the Gas Pump Lounge. "Let's dance," she added and they did.

Murphy did tell Charlie that he had never been married, "Not even close," he said, but he didn't elaborate further. Lying in bed he reasoned that the relationship was going to have to get a whole lot more serious before he brought up the "one male child named Murphy" Murphy family tradition. He drifted off to sleep reliving all the goodnight kisses and thinking he had just had the best night of his life. At that moment the case of Serious Crisis was the furthest thing from his mind. That mindset changed the very next day.

"Compared to the rest of the items yours seems a bit, can I say, inconsequential," Murphy pulled no punches. He and Jeffrey Giucigiu were seated four rows up, directly facing the arena's stage. A crew of half a dozen were lining up chairs for people to sit, floor level, but leaving a thirty-foot area right in front of the stage open. "People like to get up and dance or form a mosh pit," Giucigiu had said when Murphy asked why.

"It's not inconsequential to me," the manager responded somewhat sheepishly about his missing case of bubbly water.

"Where was it the last time you remember seeing it? Who, besides you, would have had access to it? Was it your private stash or did you share with any members of the band?"

Jeff thought for a moment. "I'm pretty sure it was either in one of the belly bays or actually on the tour bus. And, the band was certainly welcome to it but nobody else liked it."

Somebody did Murphy thought. "Belly bays?" he asked.

"The storage areas at the underside of the bus. You know, the places where Greyhound stores your luggage. It's where we put some equipment or personal belongings." Murphy nodded silently and Jeff continued, "As far as who had access? A lot of people if the case was in the bays, quite a bit fewer if it was on the bus."

"And you can't remember which of the two it was?"

"I can't."

"What happened night before last?" Murphy switched gears, "During the show at The Gas Pump Lounge?"

"Good show," Giucigiu answered. "Lots of energy and Lyndsay never sounded better."

"Not what I meant."

"What did you mean?"

"Turrell's sunglasses," Murphy clarified. "What was that all about?"

"Oh that," he replied, "That was nothing. DeMaio couldn't find his shades, claimed they weren't where they always were. Read the riot act to a couple of crew guys. Typical temperamental superstar," the manager laughed.

"Had that ever happened before?" the detective didn't share Giucigiu's amusement, "During a performance?"

"Not that I can recall. They've been doing that schtick before playing "Future So Bright" for more than a month now. It was Lyndsay's idea," he paused. "Now that you mention it, it's definitely the first time I can remember it happening."

"And you attend every show?"

"Everyone. Hear every song."

"That must get old," Murphy projected

"Actually, it doesn't. Ever. Not with this group," Jeff said proudly.

"Can you give me a good reason I shouldn't consider you a suspect?" Murphy used a technique he had learned from his Captain. Throw out a random question, or accusation, then sit back and gauge the reaction. In this case he couldn't help but notice the inquiry took the manager by surprise. In fact, Jeff looked like he'd been slapped.

"Me? A suspect? No way detective," he shot back. "These guys are my friends. Heck, you could say they're my family. This band is my life. It was that way when I first started and that feeling still persists today. I would never do anything to cause any one of them harm. Wouldn't even think of it."

Murphy couldn't believe the back to back redundancies, "That's a good reason," Murphy said, easily believing the sentiment. "Did Turrell ever find his sunglasses?" he rerouted the conversation back. Giucigiu took a deep breath.

"Not that I know of," he said, "But I'll find out."

"I think we both know the answer to that question is going to be no." Giucigiu nodded. "How many people have direct access to the band during a tour?"

The manager thought for a moment, Murphy could see him counting to himself. "Let's see," he started, "The five people in the band, me, Morris, but he's blind," he added, "and four roadies. That makes eleven."

"How long have Mr. Morrisey and the other four been with you?" Murphy was making notes.

"Mo Mo has been working the board since the first Serious Crisis tour." He released a long breath. "Which is when Smitty and Jimmy Dimsum came on board."

"Jimmy Dimsum?" Murphy looked up from his pad.

"His real name is Jim Demaret but pretty much all he eats is dim sum so…" the manager trailed off.

"And what about Roadie number three? Has he been around from the beginning? Any reason I should suspect him?"

"Her," he corrected, "Roadie number three is a her. Olive."

"Just Olive?"

"Olive Green, actually," Giucigiu answered, "and she's been around a little over a year."

"More than," Murphy corrected him

"More than what?"

"Never mind," Murphy Murphy shook his head, "So no reason to suspect Olive," he made a note. "And the fourth one?"

"Marty Kaufmann," the manager nodded, "Older guy, bit of a burn out, but he knows his way around an axe."

"Axe?" Murphy asked looking up from his notes.

"Guitar. Axe is slang for guitar," Giucigiu assured him. "The guy has a great ear. More a guitar tech than a simple roadie. Keeps both DeMaio's and Lyndsay's guitars in tune."

"How long has Marty been around and where did you find him?"

"Let me think." Giucigiu thought for a moment. "A few months. If I remember right, he came on board during the last Orlando show. He was a writer for some two-bit golf publication." The manager watched Murphy scribble something in his book. "Is that important?"

"Not sure. Everything's important until it isn't."

"Anyway, guy came up to me, introduced himself. Said he was a big fan of the band and told me he knew how to play the guitar."

"That all it takes to get brought on board?"

"Not exactly," Giucigiu rubbed his chin. "Marty said he was tired of writing articles about spoiled athletes for a rag nobody read. He wanted to run away and join the circus. That made me laugh, so I hired him on the spot."

118

"So, in your opinion it's safe to say that we can eliminate three of the road crew from suspicion."

"Just three? Why not all four?"

"Marty Kaufmann shows up out of nowhere, without experience, joins the circus, as you call it, and shortly after that things start disappearing. That sound about right, Jeff?"

"Since you put it that way."

"I'd like to talk to Marty ASAP."

"No problem," the manager said looking past Murphy and smiling. "Here comes stray dog," he blurted.

"Who?"

"Lyndsay," the manager answered while getting up to greet her. Murphy turned in his seat and saw Howlund. She wore blue jeans covered to the knees by camel colored, flat heeled, boots. A Rolling Stones t-shirt covered her torso, its huge red tongue sliding out from a top row of white teeth and equally red lips. Murphy knew it was the Rolling Stones because the shirt said so, just above the logo. Her hair was pulled back into a tight ponytail that slid through a hole in the back of a white, low profile baseball cap. An orange "T" was emblazoned on the front. She hugged the manager, who must've whispered something to her because Murphy saw Lyndsay give an almost imperceptible nod. She looked at the detective and gave a small wave. Murphy waved back.

She came over and sat in the same seat Giucigiu had just vacated. Murphy thought she smelled clean, like she had just taken a shower. Upon closer inspection, Murphy could see she wore no makeup, save for a thin coating of lip gloss. She crossed her legs so her body turned in Murphy's direction and she placed both hands on her left knee.

"Hi," she said.

"Hello Miss Howlund," Murphy returned the greeting.

"Shoot detective, please call me Lyndsay."

"Ok Lyndsay," Murphy noticed the middle finger of her left hand was picking at a cuticle on the thumb of her right hand.

"Nervous?" he asked.

"Should I be?"

"Can't imagine why," he said honestly, "Unless, of course you've done something illegal."

"Ever?" she said with a disarming smile. Murphy couldn't help but observe that she had exceptionally white teeth.

"You're going to draw blood there," Murphy's eyes directed hers to her hands.

Keith Hirshland

"Oh geez," she stopped picking. "Habit. You sound just like my mother."

"My mom used to say the same thing to me." With that, Lyndsay grabbed Murphy Murphy's left hand and gave it a once over.

"But you have beautiful nails," she complimented and released the detective's hand.

"My manicurist thanks you," he smiled. "Started getting them in college, after mom threatened to stop paying my tuition." Lyndsay laughed a little laugh. "Why did Mr. Giucigiu call you 'stray dog'?" She laughed a little harder.

"Guess it's cuz I just showed up on his doorstep one day. A guitar in my hands and a hundred songs in my head."

"How did you know where he lived?" The question elicited a third laugh.

"Not his literal doorstep, silly. His hotel room door. Serious Crisis came to town and my best friend worked the front desk at the hotel where they stayed."

"Clever." The detective truly thought it was.

"I know." She clearly thought it was as well.

"Where's home?"

121

"New London, New Hampshire," she sat up a little straighter. Proud. "Right off Interstate 89."

"I've been there," he said honestly.

"Then you know there's very little crime, houses cost a fortune, for New Hampshire that is, and the weather pretty much sucks."

"Didn't stay that long," Murphy admitted.

"It wasn't a bad place to grow up," she reflected. "Quiet, safe, good schools, and only a couple of hours, even on a bad traffic day, from Boston. Great music scene in Boston," she added. Murphy noticed she was picking at her thumb again.

"Pretty cold for golf though."

"What?" she said a little startled, "How did you know I played golf?"

"Your manager." He replied. "Jeff said the item stolen from you was a dozen golf balls," he consulted his memory. "Pro X V's or something." She giggled.

"Or something," she said.

"Do they really cost fifty dollars?"

"More than that in some high-end golf shops," she admitted, "That's why I know what happens to every single one."

"Except the twelve that went missing." It was a statement, not a question.

"Except the twelve that were stolen," she replied with a statement of her own.

"Why would anyone steal golf balls? Or bubbly water, or a bow tie, or a gosh darn whip?"

"Great questions," she agreed, "As far as my balls are concerned, all I know is it couldn't have been a player. Real golfers have too much integrity."

"Do they now?" he challenged her.

"You're darn tootin," she assured him, "And besides, these were personalized."

"They were?"

"Yep. Had 'Stray Dog' stamped across each and every one of them."

"Do you think whoever stole them knew that?"

"How would I know?"

"That was your turn to ask a good question," Murphy answered. "How well do you know Mr. Kaufmann?" He changed subjects.

"Marty? The roadie? Not that well."

"Jeff says he tunes your guitars."

"He does and he's great at it. I never have to worry when I hit the stage. He does DeMaio's too."

"Why not the others?" Murphy wondered

"Have to ask them," she answered.

"Did you know Marty had a golf connection?"

"Does he?" she replied. Murphy was unsure if that answer was an indication either way.

"He does." was all he said. Then they chatted for a few more minutes until she claimed the need to prepare for that evening's concert. Since Murphy had no idea what that entailed, he couldn't put up much of a fight. He gave her his card and when she accepted it he noticed she had indeed drawn blood from the thumb's cuticle. He told her again to get a manicure and asked her to call him if she thought of anything else. As she walked away, Murphy remembered something he wanted to ask her.

"Lyndsay," he called. She stopped and turned. "What about Mags? How well do you know *him* and what are your impressions?"

"Just like Marty, not all that well. He's a groupie. Comes to shows, buys us drinks." As she resumed her exit Murphy couldn't help but realize she had only answered the first question. He looked at his watch and it told him he still had a couple of hours to kill before he hoped to run into Johnny "Jack" Maginnes again. He was hungry, so he decided to grab a burger. On the way he called a local florist and had flowers sent to Charlie Carlucci.

Murphy Murphy Meets Mags Again For The Second Time

Murphy wisely decided against another meal prepared by Lou and went instead to his favorite hamburger joint in town, Booger's Burgers, for lunch. Booger was another former athlete turned restauranteur, who led his high school to an upset victory in the state championship many, many moons ago. The photograph on the front page of the next morning's newspaper showed the triumphant team gathered around the trophy. Front and center was the kid who had hit the winning shot, Robert "Bobby" Kite. He had a big, wide, full-toothed grin on his face, a basketball net around his neck and a huge blob of snot coming out his nose. From that day he was "Booger" Kite and he embraced the nickname with gusto.

I know a "Booger" and a "Pizzer" Murphy thought as he enjoyed a bacon cheeseburger. He treated himself to a chocolate malt instead of Booger's renowned nacho cheese fries. Hours later, lunch still heavy in his gut, he maneuvered the Le Car back to the arena. It was four fifteen. There was no sign of Maginnes, but Murphy saw a few members of the

126

road crew carrying equipment on to the platform and placing each piece in its proper spot. It was quite a bit larger than the stage at The Gas Pump Lounge. Because of this there was more "stuff", including four guitars behind where Lyndsay Howlund would stand. That was two more than she displayed a couple of nights ago. One of the new guitars was an acoustic model, Murphy was pretty sure it was a Martin. Maybe even a D-41.

Up in the catwalk, lighting technicians were positioning and repositioning spotlights. In the middle of the floor Murphy noticed a large audio mixing board, propped up on a riser, enclosed by boundary of red velvet ropes. Seated behind the console, ears covered by headphones, was a man Murphy Murphy decided had to be Morris Morrisey. That's where the detective headed.

"Friend or foe?" a booming voice called out as Murphy started to climb the handful of steps to get on to the riser. The blind man didn't turn around but he did take off his headphones, "Identify yourself," he bellowed.

"I'm a friend," Murphy said, "At least I hope I am. Name's Murphy."

"Come on up my new friend. Have a seat next to Mo Mo." Murphy did. "How long you been a cop?" Mo Mo asked as Murphy sat.

"How do you know I'm a cop?"

"Can smell 'em a mile away. That's the consequence of having two of them beat the sight out of you. The other senses compensate."

"I'm sorry about what happened to you," Murphy said sincerely.

"Why?" Mo Mo asked. "Did you do the beatin? Did your brother, or old man?"

"No, sir," Murphy stammered out, "but—"

"No buts," Mo Mo placed his hand on Murphy's knee. "Not your fault. Not your business to apologize. Now, what can Morris Morrisey do for you officer?"

"Actually, I'm a detective," Murphy replied out of instinct, "and I'm looking into the curious case of all the band's items that have recently gone missing."

"Crazy thing that is, isn't it?"

"Very odd," Murphy agreed

"I'll ask again," Mo Mo started, "What can I do for you?"

"Maybe just answer a few questions," Murphy offered, "If you don't mind."

"Don't mind at all. You have my undivided attention until, that is, somebody in the band needs it more than you."

"Fair enough. Has there been anything stolen from *you?*" Murphy posed his first question.

"How would *I* know?" Mo Mo answered with a deep, mesmerizing, laugh. "You may have noticed I'm blind. Are you sure you're a detective?" He laughed that laugh again.

"Quite sure," Murphy laughed too. "How much time do you spend around the band? Have you heard anything about the missing items? Has anyone in the band confided in you?"

"Three questions at once," Mo Mo chided the detective. "Quite a bit. No and no." Murphy leaned back and figured he had crossed Mo Mo off the suspect list for good reason. Then he thought of something else.

"Friend of mine says you sometimes drive the tour bus. That true?" A smile spread across Morris Morrisey's face.

"Ssshhh," he put a wrinkled, slightly bent, forefinger to his lips, "Not so loud detective. I would hate for your comrades in the Highway Patrol to find out."

"You mean it's true?"

"Sure, it's true." Mo Mo assured him, "But only on the straight roads." He slapped Murphy on the back and roared with laughter. Just then DeMaio Turrell wandered onto the stage wearing, what looked to Murphy Murphy like a brand-new pair of sunglasses.

At the same time Johnny "Jack" Maginnes walked through one of the arena's side doors. Same white shirt under the same Hawaiian shirt. Different, darker cargo shorts and running shoes over short socks.

"Mind if I hang out here for a minute?"

"Don't mind a bit, stay as long as you like. But you might want to grab a pair of those." He pointed to a box filled with orange foam ear plugs. "It's about to get a little noisy in here."

Murphy thought back to just a couple of afternoons before and remembered not needing ear protection for the soundcheck. *Maybe it's the heightened sense of hearing thing* he thought. But this time there was no thump, thump, thump from Herbie Albanese's kick drum. Instead his ears were assaulted by one hundred and twenty decibels of screaming instruments. Murphy instantly reached for the foam plugs and shoved one in each ear. Mo Mo gave him a smile and a thumbs up. The noise lasted less than a couple of minutes, but to Murphy it felt like two minutes underwater. Finally, it stopped.

"What was *that*?" Murphy yelled. Mo Mo, who had one ear exposed, answered but Murphy couldn't hear him. *Oh great,* the detective thought, *he's blind and now I'm deaf.* Then he remembered the ear plugs and pulled them out. "What was that?" he asked again.

"That," Mo Mo said, "was Serious Crisis having a little fun."

After another fifteen minutes of "Mo Mo could I get a little more of this" or "a little less of that", the band settled into a rhythm and rehearsed a few songs. Satisfied, at least for now, they all thanked the engineer and started to fiddle with their various instruments. Herbie, the drummer, jumped off the stage and greeted Maginnes with some sort of special handshake. Murphy didn't want the man to disappear again so he offered his own thanks to Morris and headed toward Mags.

"Johnny 'Jack' Maginnes," Murphy approached from behind after Herbie Albanese had left.

"Well done, detective," Mags said without turning around. "I see you're still writing that book."

"What's an ex-Navy seal, former cop, and current sherlock doing stalking a rock 'n roll band?" Murphy got right to the point.

"I take exception to the characterization." he still faced away from Murphy, "I prefer 'inquiry agent' or even 'detective'," he finally turned, "Just like you."

"Why are you here, Johnny? Why were you at The Gas Pump Lounge? Why have you been to every Serious Crisis show for the past three months?"

"Four," he corrected, "And *that,* detective, is none of your business."

"Why did you bolt the other night? During the commotion surrounding DeMaio Turrell's sunglasses?" Murphy pressed on. "Or is that also none of my business?"

"You ask a lot of questions and yes, it's none of your business."

"Humor me," Murphy implored, "Or better yet, show me some professional courtesy."

Maginnes rolled his eyes. "If you must know I had a call about another case. Needed some privacy and a quieter setting."

Murphy smiled, just a little. "So, this obsession with musicians less than half your age is actually a case." Murphy noticed a slight change in the private investigator's demeanor.

"Didn't say that." Maginnes seemed to regain his composure.

"You said *another* case."

"I'm working a lot of cases, detective, which are also none of your business."

"Clearly I'm in the wrong business," Murphy smiled at Mags. "Why didn't you come back to the show once what is none of my business was concluded?"

"Why so many questions about the other night?" Johnny sounded annoyed.

"Did you steal Turrell's sunglasses?" Murphy went with the same approach he had tried on Lyndsay Howlund earlier.

"Ahhh," Maginnes nodded, "The old 'ask an accusatory question out of the blue' trick. Has that worked well for you in the past Mr. Murphy? By the way, since we've become so close, can I call you by your first name?"

"If you'd like."

"Great. What is it?"

"It's Murphy"

"No, your first name."

"It's Murphy," he repeated

"Whatever," Maginnes said, turning back toward the stage.

"Did you steal Mr. Turrell's sunglasses?"

Maginnes laughed out loud. "I sure did!" his fake confession dripping with sarcasm, "Excellent police work, detective. I pilfered a pair of sunglasses right out from under the band's nose and snuck out into the night and sold them on the street corner. Got a hundred bucks." He put both hands behind his back, "Cuff me. Take me in."

"I'm told they were worth four times that." Murphy was pretty sure Maginnes didn't take the glasses. His jury was still out with regard to the other items. "Someone took advantage of you."

"That would be a first," Johnny 'Jack' Maginnes sounded as if he had never spoken truer words.

"Why the fascination with this particular band?" Murphy circled back

"Again," Maginnes held Murphy's gaze, "that is none of your business."

For the second time in three nights Murphy Murphy watched Serious Crisis perform. The arena show was different in so many ways from the private concert, only the names of the songs were the same. Under the bright lights DeMaio Turrell strutted and sang, strummed his guitar and seduced his audience. Murphy had seen Springsteen, Wilco, The Rolling Stones, and a few others live and felt Serious Crisis, while not yet in that league, was well on their way and worthy of all the critical acclaim. He understood why his friend Judith was a fan and wondered if she was one of the thousands in the audience using the flashlight function on their smartphones as an electronic candle, hoping to convince the band to reappear for a third encore. After several minutes Murphy knew that effort was in vain.

He had long since lost sight of Mags and didn't really care. The private investigator was up to something but robbing a rock band wasn't it. He was much more interested in the roadie, Marty Kaufmann, so he thanked Mo Mo again and stood.

"See you down the road Detective Murphy," Morris said with a smile. Murphy smiled back.

"Looking forward to it," he replied sincerely and headed toward the stage. He passed two members of the crew he knew to be Olive and Smitty. Olive because she was a woman and Smitty because he wore a "Serious Crisis Crew" black t-shirt with the word "Smitty" emblazoned on the back. That left the guy they called Jimmy Dimsum and Marty Kaufmann. One of them was taking apart Herbie Albanese's drum kit while the other, his back to Murphy, was kneeling near Lyndsay Howlund's guitars. Murphy headed for the guitars.

"Mr. Kaufmann?" Murphy approached. Kaufmann stood and turned toward the sound. Murphy noticed he was wearing what appeared to be expensive sunglasses. The detective held out his shield.

"Mr. Kaufmann is my father, God rest his soul," Kaufmann crossed himself. "I'm Marty."

"Fair enough Marty," Murphy replied, "I'm detective Murphy. I have a few questions."

"Not a problem but can you ask them while I load out? We're on a bit of a schedule."

"How long have you been with the band?"

"Hah!" Kaufmann laughed out loud, "That's an interesting way of putting it."

"What do you mean?"

"Well if you haven't noticed," Kaufmann held up both guitars, "I'm not exactly *with* the band. I load and unload their equipment, tune their guitars, and clean up the stage after they make a mess."

"You sound a little bitter."

"Do I?"

"Isn't that what a guitar tech does?" Murphy asked. "Isn't that what you signed up for?" he added.

"Well, sure," Kaufmann conceded. "I'm well aware that hindsight is 20/20 when you look back." Murphy's mouth dropped open. "But a guy can dream, can't he?" Murphy didn't say a word. He expected the man to keep on talking, despite the concern that more redundancies would come forth. He had interviewed guys like Marty Kaufmann before, guys that wanted to get something off their chests. "Look, detective, I didn't mean to sound bitter. The band is great, the pay's not bad and I get to see the world." He lifted Lyndsay's guitars and started walking away. Murphy followed.

"It's just that I'm a pretty good guitar player myself," he said over his shoulder. "Not as good as Turrell but—"

"Better than Lyndsay." Murphy finished his sentence.

"Way better," he confirmed. "Don't get me wrong, she's good and she has terrific equipment."

"Especially the Martin," the detective prodded.

"Yeah," the roadie said wistfully, "Especially the D-41."

"But I suppose the bottom line is you aren't quite as pretty as Miss Howlund," Murphy countered.

"And therein lies the rub," Kaufmann agreed.

"What do you know about the band's missing items?" Murphy asked. Kaufmann stopped and turned.

"Not too much. I know they're missing," he answered and started walking again.

"What kind of golf balls do you use Mister Kaufmann?" Murphy sensed the question caught the roadie by surprise.

"When I play, which isn't all that often anymore, I use whatever I find." He turned again, "Golf balls are expensive detective."

"Where did you get the sunglasses, Marty?" Again, a beat before an answer.

"DeMaio gave them to me," he finally said.

"Did he now?"

But the rush of adrenaline and excitement in thinking he was on to something soon faded. Murphy and Marty found DeMaio Turrell and confirmed that the lead singer had indeed given the thought lost sunglasses to the roadie.

"The company somehow heard that I had lost them," Turrell told Murphy Murphy. "So they sent me a new pair. In the meantime we found the old ones in the bus so I gave them to Marty."

"Those are three hundred-dollar shades," Murphy chastised the singer, "You just left them lying around the bus?" Turrell shrugged his shoulders. Kaufmann actually coughed when he heard the price tag.

"This guy does a hell of a job tuning my axe," DeMaio tilted his head toward the roadie. "My way of saying thanks." Kaufmann put his hands together as is in prayer and bowed to the band's front man.

The chat with DeMaio Turrell alleviated some of the suspicion Murphy had about Kaufmann, but not all of it. So the detective asked the roadie to show him his living arrangements. Without objection he led Murphy to a smaller, older bus. Inside Kaufmann pointed out his sleeping quarters. Murphy noticed a small bed in an only slightly bigger room. It could be closed off by a curtain and it was right next to an identical space that was clearly occupied by Smitty. He was sitting on his own bed picking at a banjo.

Across the narrow hallway Murphy saw an identical set up with two more rooms. He figured those belonged to Olive and Jimmy Dimsum. There was a railing above Kaufmann's bed that held a medium sized suitcase. Murphy asked the roadie to get it down and he did. Inside were a couple of pairs of jeans, some t-shirts, one sweatshirt, socks, underwear and a pair of cargo shorts. There were no bowties, no golf balls, and there was certainly no whip. Murphy Murphy concluded that there was also no privacy.

There was a small cardboard box filled with books. The detective noticed mostly mysteries, some by authors he knew and also read; Michael Connelly, David Baldacci, Christopher Moore. There was one titled *The Flower Girl Murder* by a guy Murphy had never heard of.

After an hour or so, and conversations with Smitty and Olive, Murphy decided Marty Kaufmann was who he said he was, just a guy with a dream of being a rock star. It meant that the guitar tech was a dead end.

He went home to get some much needed sleep, too tired for tea or Mozart. His head hit the pillow thinking about going into the precinct in the morning to start his "crime book". It was a process he had adopted of putting all his notes, thoughts, and relevant information into the computer using a chronological timeline. He'd label this one The Case of Serious Crisis.

Night Turned To Day, Then Day Turned Back To Night Again

Writing was exactly what he was doing when the phone at his desk rang the next morning. Ready for a break he picked it up.

"Murphy," he said.

"Hey Murph." It was Judith Colman.

"Hey Jude, what's up? Why are you calling on this line?"

"Tried your mobile, went straight to voicemail. This was option number two." Murphy looked at his phone and realized it was dead.

"Geez, looks like I forgot to charge it," he said to himself and to Judith. "Some detective."

"I was just wondering if you wanted to head to the park with me and the pups," she said, ignoring his self-criticism.

"Sounds great," he replied. "I need a break both from and in this case."

"So let's walk and talk," she offered, "See if something shakes loose."

"See you in fifteen."

They strolled along the river. Murphy had Bear on a leash while Judith was responsible for Namath who, despite being off leash, stayed close.

"The city has a leash law you know," the detective said offhandedly.

"Well then come a little closer so I can hook you up," Judith replied.

"I just can't get a grip on this case," Murphy knew he would get nowhere with the leash conversation. "I thought I had two really solid leads, the groupie and a guitar tech slash roadie, but as of last night it appears neither is worth pursuing. I feel like I'm back at square one."

"Until you're sure about both, don't give up on either," Judith said prophetically.

"That's smart." Murphy knew her advice was sound. They walked a bit in silence.

"A guitar tech?" Judith broke it.

"Guy named Marty Kaufmann. Joined the parade a few months ago, shortly before the stuff started to disappear."

"That sounds like an amazing coincidence."

"Exactly what I thought, but when I looked closer it just seemed there was no way he could be the thief."

"Why?"

"He lives on a bus in close quarters with others. The road crew that's been with the band for a while has zero privacy. No place to hide anything."

"There's *always* a place to hide something," Judith said cryptically.

"Plus DeMaio Turrell vouched for the guy." Namath suddenly became more interested in a squirrel than his master's conversation and he headed for a tree.

"Joe Willie!" Judith raised her voice and the dog put on the brakes. "Get back here, you've got no shot." The dog returned.

"Never knew his full name," Murphy said, patting the dog on the head.

"Roll Tide," she laughed in response. "So, what's your next move?" she asked, bringing the conversation back to the case.

"I'm going back to the station to work on the crime notebook. See if anything jogs my memory. As much as I enjoyed the music, I'd really like to not have to go back and see the band perform again." He was referring to Serious Crisis's third and final show this trip to town.

"I'm going tonight."

"That's right. I remember you said you had tickets."

"Maybe Charlie and I could do some snooping around. On your behalf, of course."

"Charlie?" Murphy stopped. Judith took a couple more steps before stopping too.

"Charlie Carlucci. I talked her in to going to the show with me." She smiled.

"Great. Have fun," Murphy smiled back, "I'm sure snooping around will be on the agenda."

"No doubt about that." She started walking again.

Murphy went back to work. He thought for a second about calling Charlie Carlucci. He even picked up the phone and punched in the first few digits. Then, wondering if sending flowers had been the wrong move, decided against completing the call.

He sat behind his desk and went back over the notebook from the beginning. Murphy remembered Judith saying that "there's always some place to hide something" and he hung on to those words as he went back through the case. Nothing jumped out at him but he decided Judith was right, maybe it was too early to give up on both Johnny "Jack" Maginnes or Marty Kaufmann as suspects. He also figured another go at Jeffrey Giucigiu shouldn't be out of the question. He worked for hours; adding and subtracting notes, retracing his steps, recalling conversations and interviews. The sun had long since set and Murphy's stomach reminded him that it had been a while since he ate. He also thought a Jameson sounded good so he wrapped up, locked up, and headed toward Bar Flight. He knew Judith wasn't there, but he hoped the Pizzer was. Richie Pizzoni was usually good for a laugh.

The neon light was on at the pub, except the "l" of course. Murphy opened the door and was greeted by a smiling Buck.

"Evening Buck," he said what he always said, "What's shakin'?" he added what he hardly ever said. Murphy pulled his right hand from his coat pocket and offered it to Buck.

"Detective," the bouncer answered grasping Murphy's hand with his own. "No Miss Colman tonight."

"Yep, I know. Is the Pizzer behind the bar?"

"Sure is," Buck scowled, "And that's why nobody's in front of it." His scowl became a smile.

"Think he can handle a Jameson on the rocks?" Murphy smiled back.

"I'd put those odds at 50-50," Buck said and the smile turned into a full-throated laugh. Murphy went in.

Two TV's had some basketball game on, two others showed *Eddie and the Cruisers*. The sound from those sets bounced around the mostly empty bar. Eddie, Sal Amato and Joann Carlino were singing "Down On My Knees". Murphy sidled up to the bar.

"Slow night?" he asked the owner.

"Is now," Pizzoni shot back. "Had a bunch of nitwits in here a while ago. The whole bunch of them asking for foo foo drinks." The Pizzer shook his head in disbelief and wiped the bar in front of Murphy with a damp rag. "What the heck is a Kir Royale anyway?" Murphy thought it was champagne with a splash of Chambord, but he guessed Judith would know for sure.

"How about a Jameson rocks," he said to Pizzoni, "And what's the dinner special?"

"Lou's one of a kind Shepherd's Pie," Richie answered, reaching for a glass and the bottle of whiskey. "It's none too bad. I've only had to hit the head once since I ate." He winked at Murphy.

"Now that's what I call a ringing endorsement," the detective concluded, "I'll try it but you better make that Jameson a double."

"Comin right up!" the Pizzer shouted with an ear to ear grin.

Murphy was a sip or two away from finishing his first Irish Whiskey and halfway through Lou's

146

Shepherd's Pie. The first game had ended and a second one was starting. In the movie, Joann had just revealed she was the one who took the master tapes of The Cruisers' second album from Satin records and hid them in the Palace of Depression.

"How's the pie?" It was Lou.

"Actually not bad," Murphy admitted. "Do I taste a hint of Worcestershire?"

"Secret ingredient," Lou's smile showed three missing teeth, "Nicely done detective." The cook started walking back to the kitchen.

"That's why I make the big bucks," Murphy said to Lou's back. Richie Pizzoni refilled Murphy's water glass and his whiskey. "Hey Richie, do you know where the phrase 'belly up the bar' came from?"

"Maybe."

"Well, I heard it started because saloon owners back in the day didn't want a bunch of drunk kids running around town, so your belly had to reach the height of the bar to get a drink." Murphy took another bite of his dinner. Pizzoni stared at him for a good twenty seconds. "What?" Murphy asked mid-chew.

"That's complete B.S." the bar owner finally spoke. "What if you were a midget, or a really tall kid for that matter? Your theory goes down for the count."

"Not my theory," Murphy said defensively, "I just heard it and was asking you if you thought it was true."

"Whoever said it was making it way too complicated. In the old days bars had no stools, either couldn't afford 'em and the one's that could got tired of folks breaking them over each other." Murphy listened intently. "So, if you wanted a drink," Pizzoni continued, "you just had to stand close to the bar, put your belly up to it, so to speak."

"I like my theory better," Murphy chided.

"Not surprised," Pizzoni snapped the bar rag at the detective, "But your theory is hogwash."

Back home, Murphy settled into his favorite chair as Mozart's *Concerto for Violin and Orchestra No. 3 in G* played from the speakers. Murphy thought about Marty Kaufmann, since he still wanted to like him for the robberies. "There's always some place to hide something," he said to the night. *Maybe Kaufmann used one of the belly bays in the older bus to stash his stolen goods. Did the roadie bus even have belly bays?* Murphy made a mental note to find out. *Was there an extra guitar case somewhere? All of the stolen items would easily fit in one of those.* He made another note. *Giucigiu said Kaufmann joined the band in Orlando after quitting his job at a golf magazine. How many of those can there be? Does he still have an address in Orlando, a post office box? A place to stash stuff?*

More notes to remember, more boxes to check, more phone calls to make. Murphy liked where this was going, and he could feel a rhythm coming back to the case. From experience he knew as long as there were more questions than answers a lead was never completely cold. He smiled, thinking he had work to do. An early morning would send him back over to the arena to ask more questions and get a more thorough look at the roadie bus. He programmed his MacIntosh receiver to sleep in a couple of hours and he closed his eyes. He listened to Mozart, and thought about all the ways Marty Kaufmann could have ripped off Serious Crisis.

Sometime later the phone rang Murphy awake. He looked around, momentarily disoriented, until he realized he had fallen asleep in the chair. A glance at the ringing phone's screen told the detective it was 5:40 in the morning. Before the call went to voicemail he answered.

"Murphy."

"Detective. Sorry to call so early in the morning," Murphy recognized the voice of Jeff Giucigiu, "but I'm afraid we possibly might have a problem."

"We or you?" Murphy asked, angered over the redundancy.

"We. That is, if you are still interested in trying to help solve the case."

"Okay, what's our problem?" Murphy asked, "Has something else been stolen?"

"Not exactly stolen."

"Please get to the point, Jeff. What *exactly* has not exactly been stolen?"

"Lyndsay's Martin D-41," he said, "And it's more like missing."

"Good grief!" Murphy's thoughts went immediately to Kaufmann, "Why do you say it's more like missing?"

"Because we can't find Lyndsay or Marty Kaufmann either." It sounded to Murphy like Giucigiu was crying.

"And you chose to lead with the guitar?" Murphy was incredulous.

"And tell him my new pair of glasses are gone too!" the detective heard DeMaio Turrell in the background. "Shut up Walter," Giucigiu said.

"I'll be right there," Murphy disconnected and headed for a quick shower.

Murphy Murphy rolled up to the arena in the LeCar. It was 6:45. Both busses were parked near the loading dock, Murphy could see Jeff Giucigiu and another man standing by the roadie bus talking. The detective parked his official vehicle in the loading zone and walked over to the two men.

"Nice ride," the man Murphy didn't know said, "Very official."

"You must be Jimmy Dimsum," Murphy didn't take the bait. "Jeff," he said to the manager.

"I must be," Dimsum said. Murphy pulled his note pad from a back pocket and flipped it to an open page.

"Old school," Jimmy smiled.

"Tell me what happened," Murphy ignored the roadie and spoke to Giucigiu.

"I got a call from Jimmy at 5:15. He said there was a problem and I needed to come down to the arena right away."

"Did he say why?"

"I'm right here boss," Dimsum objected.

"He did not," Jeff answered Murphy.

"I did not," the roadie echoed.

"Why not?" this time Murphy turned his attention to Jimmy.

"Too hard to explain over the phone."

"Why 5:15?" Murphy continued. "What was going on at that time of the morning?"

"Pulling out," Jimmy replied.

"At 5:15? Why so early?"

"That's our usual habit. We do it the same identical way every time."

"Good Lord," Murphy said under his breath as Dimsum continued.

"We like to hit the road early. Less traffic, fewer knuckleheads."

"Who drives?"

"Usually me," the roadie said.

"Never Mo Mo?" Murphy asked.

"What?" the roadie looked at Murphy like he had three eyeballs.

"Never mind," Murphy smiled, "Go on."

"I get a good night's sleep the night before we're on the move. The other guys do the load out on the last night in a city. Then they sleep while I drive."

"When did you notice something was amiss?"

"Amiss? Mo Mo driving? Man, you are a trip."

"Please answer the question."

"I dunno, five am. Maybe a few minutes earlier. I checked the bays on both busses, since it's my job to double check that all the gear is stored properly."

"There are bays on the roadie bus?"

"Of course," Dimsum snorted, "It's a bus."

"Do each of you have your own bay? For storing personal items?"

"No way man," Jimmy shook his head, "Nowhere near enough room for that. The four of us share one bay."

"Ok, we'll come back to that. You checked the bays on this bus and that's when you noticed Lyndsay's Martin wasn't loaded?"

"Not *this* bus," he pointed a nail chewed finger at the older vehicle, "*That* one." His finger went to Serious Crisis's bus. "She keeps that baby close and sometimes their bus and ours aren't even in the same time zone."

"Who loaded Lyndsay's guitars on the other bus?"

"Used to be Olive, now most nights it's Marty's job. It was again last night."

"What changed?"

"Marty got hired. I guess Lyndsay liked the way he tuned and treated her equipment."

"Was Olive upset?"

"Not at all," Dimsum announced without thinking. "Lyndsay could be very protective of her guitars, especially that D-41. Anyway she told me last night she took care of Herbie's drum kit while Smitty handled Big Joe's and Chuckie's stuff. Marty was Lyndsay's guy."

"Was there more to their relationship than just taking care of her stuff on stage?"

"Not that I'm aware of," the roadie shook his head again, "And that kind of thing would be pretty hard to hide around here."

"Did you know Marty played the guitar? Wanted to be in the band?"

"Dude, *everybody* plays the guitar, and in case you hadn't noticed, a lot of people want to be in the band."

"Even you?"

"Nah, not me. I got no musical aptitude. I just like the girls and the chance to eat dim sum all over the world. I'm writing a book." The statement made Murphy think of Johnny "Jack" Maginnes.

"Is the book about the girls or the dumplings?" he asked.

"Both," Jimmy laughed.

"No stories about the band?"

"No way!" Dimsum shook his head. "Wouldn't want to say anything that might get me fired."

"Back to Lyndsay's guitar. You said you noticed it missing around five?"

"Close proximity to that," Jimmy answered. Murphy rolled his eyes.

"And then you did what?"

"Well, as quietly as I could, I went into her bus to see if she had it with her."

"You have a key to the band's bus?" Murphy pointed his pen at the bus.

"Sure, we all do," Jimmy nodded, "Just in case." Murphy made a note.

"And there was no guitar."

"No guitar and no Lyndsay."

"Is it your habit to peek into Miss Howlund's sleeping quarters?"

"What? No! What kind of question is that? Lyndsay usually sleeps on the couch near the front of the cab. Told me one time she can't sleep in the back with Big Joe snoring like a locomotive."

"That a fact?" Murphy was skeptical, so he asked Giucigiu.

"That's a fact," the manager confirmed. Murphy made another note.

"Ok, so the guitar seems to be gone. Lyndsay seems to be gone. You notice anything else missing?"

"Just Marty," Dimsum added. "When I came back to our bus to see if anyone knew anything, I noticed Kaufmann's bunk hadn't been slept in. That's when I called Jeff."

"I came right over to look around," the manager chimed in, "And then I called you."

"Over from where?" Murphy asked.

"The hotel. I don't sleep on the bus."

"By the way, where's Mr. Morrisey?" Murphy finally realized he hadn't seen the sound engineer.

"He doesn't sleep on the bus either," Giucigiu said.

"Let me see your phone," the detective addressed the roadie again.

"What for?" he protested.

"Just give it to him," Giucigiu semi-ordered. Dimsum reached into his pocket for the device and handed it to Murphy.

"Unlock it," he requested. Dimsum did. Murphy scrolled through the recent activity and noticed both calls and texts to Howlund and Kaufmann. "You called and texted both Lyndsay and Marty this morning," he looked at Jimmy, "Why didn't you mention that?"

"Slipped my mind, I guess. Besides, neither answered."

"What now?" Giucigiu interrupted.

"Now we wake everybody else up," the detective said, tossing the phone back to Dimsum.

Murphy quickly came to the conclusion that the band didn't know very much about what happened to their missing member. Mostly because that's what they all said. Turrell, Lionns and Gruber, through sleepy voices, claimed to have left the arena to attend an after party. They added there were dozens of witnesses and Big Joe even showed Murphy Murphy Uber receipts on his phone. Murphy scribbled a note that Lionns had been dropped off and picked up, but he would talk to someone at the party to see if the others were with him. They all added they were a little too drunk and a lot too tired to notice if Lyndsay was on the bus when they returned. Herbie Albanese had a much more solid alibi. The drummer claimed to have spent the night, in his "room" on the bus, with a lady friend.

"She's still in there, asleep, if you need to talk to her." Murphy assured Albanese that the only reason he might have to talk to her was to ask if she heard Lyndsay, Kaufmann or anything out of the ordinary.

The drummer assured the detective they had not. "I had the music turned up pretty loud," he added sheepishly.

"When was the last time any of you saw Lyndsay, Marty, or the guitar?" Murphy asked the group.

"What guitar?" Big Joe wanted to know.

"Not yours," Jeff Giucigiu answered, "None of yours," he assured the rest.

"The Martin D-41," Murphy clarified and then asked again, "When was the last time you saw it? Or them?"

"That guitar is hardcore," Turrell said to the morning air, "I guess the last time I saw stray dog or Marty was around midnight," he spoke directly to Murphy, "Maybe a little before." Big Joe and Gruber nodded in unison.

"Right after the show," added Herbie, "Like I said, I had company."

"Okay, I'm gonna need everybody to hang tight and stay clear of both busses while I have a forensics team come take a look." There were howls of protest.

"How long will that take?" Dimsum asked, "We gotta roll."

"What you gotta do is hold your horses. This is a potential crime scene."

"Is that really necessary?" Giucigiu came to Jimmy's defense.

"Has Lyndsay Howlund gone missing before?" was all Murphy had to say in response.

Murphy knew the techs would come up empty. More specifically they would encounter a forensics smorgasbord. Too many people had access to both busses on a regular basis, meaning fingerprints and DNA belonging to everybody associated with the band would be everywhere. Including the couch on which Lyndsay Howlund reportedly spent most of her nights. Regardless, he had to call them just in case he got lucky and to cover his butt. He told Jimmy his colleagues wouldn't be there long, once they arrived, and he could be on the road sooner rather than later. Murphy had no idea if what he said was true. Out of courtesy, when he made the call, he requested the team look at the roadie bus first. Before leaving Murphy learned the band was headed west for shows in Tennessee, Kentucky, and Ohio. Giucigiu said those shows would go on with or without Lyndsay Howlund and her Martin guitar. He added he thought they'd be okay for a while with one less member of the road crew. The manager and the detective promised to stay in constant touch.

Back downtown, Murphy added the notes and pictures he had taken to the book. He remembered how Kaufmann had hitched his wagon to the group in Orlando, Florida. Murphy and an Orlando P.D.

detective had become friends at a law enforcement convention years earlier. He scrolled through the contacts in his phone until he found who he was looking for and hit the call button.

"Turner," the Florida detective answered on the third ring.

"Mal, it's Murphy Murphy."

"Detective Murphy," Mal Turner answered warmly, "Long time, no talk." Murphy knew one of the benefits of having the same first and last names was people tended not to forget him. But there was more to the connection with Turner than that. They met the first evening of the cop convention at a cocktail reception and hit it off. They had similar views on law enforcement, criminals, and police procedure.

"That's all on me," Murphy apologized for the lack of correspondence, "No excuse."

"Don't remember dialing your number recently," Turner shouldered some of the blame. "Good to hear from you. What's up?"

"I'm taking a flyer here," Murphy went on to tell his counterpart how he got involved in the Serious Crisis case, "I'm looking for a former resident of your fine city. Guy named Marty Kaufmann," he said at the end.

"The golf writer?"

"You know him?" Murphy couldn't hide his surprise.

"I do. In fact, I played golf with him a time or two."

"I didn't know you were a golfer," Murphy said, "You any good?"

"Nobody's any good," Turner laughed, "Golf is hard. But Marty wasn't bad. I remember he was a Titleist guy through and through."

"What does that mean?"

"All his equipment was from one company, Titleist. Clubs, balls, bag, even his shoes were FootJoys. He told me he had a good buddy who was one of their equipment reps. Is that important?"

"Not sure," Murphy answered, "When I asked him about golf he said he only played occasionally and the balls he used were whichever ones he could find in the woods."

"That's not the Marty Kaufmann I know. He teed it up at least twice a week and only played Pro V 1's."

"Interesting," Murphy said because he thought it was.

"Forgive me but I'm a little confused. What does golf equipment used by an Orlando golf writer have to do with items stolen from a rock n roll band?"

"Kaufmann isn't an Orlando golf writer any longer," Murphy connected the dots for his friend, "He's now part of the Serious Crisis road crew and now he happens to be missing."

"Holy cow!" Turner blurted, "And you like him for the robberies?"

"I don't dislike him for them but as you can imagine I have a lot more questions than answers."

"Now that I think of it I'm not all that surprised he quit or lost his job."

"Why do you say that?" Murphy was taking notes again.

"A little while ago he wrote a scathing cover story for his magazine about Tiger Woods and the way a few of the talking heads and the management of The Golf Network slobbered all over him."

"There's a Golf Network?" Murphy asked and heard Turner laugh out loud again.

"For about twenty years, Murphy. Where have you been?"

"I don't watch golf."

"Clearly. Anyway, Marty hammered them pretty good and word around the practice tees was that the big wigs at The Golf Network called for the magazine to cut him loose."

"They can do that?"

"The camera is king," Mal said in response, "And magazines, especially niche ones, are dying."

"I had no idea."

"That's because you spend most of your free time with a composer who's been dead for almost three hundred years." Murphy had mentioned that he was a huge classical music fan, especially Mozart.

"I'm working to remedy that."

"Good for you," the detective said to the detective. "Anyway, the golf magazine guys are falling all over themselves to become TV guys, so if someone in power at the network says 'jump', it's not surprising the mag guys say 'how high'."

"Apparently 'how high' was the low point for Marty Kaufmann."

"Apparently."

"Is he still in your system? Does he still have a place there?"

"Don't know but it's easy to find out. Give me some time."

"Take all the time you need," Murphy said, "But hurry," he added

"Roger that," Turner hung up. Murphy added a few more notes to the Marty Kaufmann section of the book. His phone rang and without looking, he answered.

"That was quick."

"What was quick?" Judith Colman asked

"Oh, hey Jude. Sorry, I thought you were someone else."

"I'm not."

"How are you?" Murphy asked, realizing Judith sounded grouchy. "How was the concert last night?"

"Don't you mean how's Charlie?"

"Maybe," Murphy couldn't lie to her.

"She's good. I'm good," Murphy hoped his honesty softened her. "The show was really, really good."

"Did you happen to notice anything odd or surprising about Lyndsay Howlund or anybody around her?" Murphy brought the conversation back to the case.

"Odd how? Surprising in what way?" She asked. "On the contrary, Lyndsay seemed dialed in last night. She killed it. They all did."

"She's missing."

"What?"

"Yep, sometime either just before or just after midnight best we can tell. Lyndsay, her acoustic guitar, and one of the roadies are all missing."

"The older one with the longish hair?" Her question made Murphy picture Kaufmann.

"That's the guy."

"He did seem to be around quite a bit more than what I would think was normal. Taking and tuning her guitars between almost every song. A couple times she seemed pissed."

"You could see all that?"

"We were four rows from the front on her side of the stage," she answered, "Hard not to see it."

"Huh," was all Murphy said.

"Do you think he did something to her?"

"Not sure. I'm thinking about going to Orlando to snoop around. That's where he lived before he joined the band."

"I love Orlando," Judith exclaimed

"You do?"

"Damn skippy. The Snowbirds, the traffic, Mickey and Minnie, what's not to love?"

"The snowbirds, the traffic, Mickey and Minnie," Murphy answered simply.

"She likes you," Judith said.

"Minnie?"

"No silly, Charlie," Judith couldn't see it but Murphy blushed. "She said it had been a while since a cute guy sent her flowers."

"Oh shoot! I meant to call her," Murphy remembered.

"You should do that."

"I will, thanks. And if you think of anything else about the concert let me know."

"You got it," Judith disconnected the call.

She likes me Murphy thought and smiled.

His daydreaming was cut short by the simultaneous ringing of the phone in his pocket and the one on his desk. The desk phone showed the call was from upstairs, Captain Hill's extension. A look at his mobile revealed a 407 area code, so he let that one go to voicemail.

"Murphy," he said answering the other one.

"Detective, the Captain would like to see you in his office."

"Right now?"

"Do you have something better to do? Yes, now."

On the way upstairs Murphy pondered what it meant that Captain Hill's assistant, Marcia, had called and not the boss himself. He was also curious why she was always so ill-tempered. Ultimately, he decided neither thing mattered.

"Go on in detective, they're expecting you," Marcia said without looking up. Murphy wondered who "they" were. He didn't have to wonder long. It took him a second but he recognized Johnny "Jack" Maginnes. Mags had cut his hair, shaved, and wore a pair of pressed khakis and a white polo shirt. He stood near the coffee maker in Hill's office and poured milk into a cup.

"Murphy," the Captain sat at his desk, "I believe you know Mr. Maginnes."

"Yes sir," Murphy answered, "Hello there Mags." Maginnes chuckled.

"Please call me John."

"Have a seat, gentlemen," the Captain pointed to a small round table and got up from behind his desk. "Let's chat." They all sat.

"What's the latest on your case?" Hill asked Murphy.

"Why is *he* here?" the detective asked instead of answering, "Who is this guy?"

"You know who I am," Maginnes answered. "I'm a private investigator and the rest, as I've told you, is pretty much none of your business."

"How about we put our pistols back in our pockets boys," Hill tried to diffuse the situation, "As of this moment we are all on the same team."

"I don't need a teammate," Murphy was defiant

"Because you've made so much progress to date?" Maginnes poked at the detective.

"As a matter of fact I have. About to head to Orlando to chase down a lead."

"Like I always say, nothing says solving a case like a visit to the Magic Kingdom."

"Gentlemen!" Captain Hill raised his voice.

"What's going on here Cap?" Murphy asked. "Seriously, who is this guy and what is he doing here?"

"What's going on here detective is that in the beginning I thought this was the perfect case for your one-man band department. The name of the rock band, the inanity of some of the things that were stolen. It all fit and I thought the length of time it would take you to solve it would be brief in duration." Murphy listened, unsure where this was headed but not liking the trip so far. "Now my niece is missing and this case has taken on a decidedly different life, a new urgency." The Captain paused and sucked in a deep breath, out of the corner of his eye Murphy noticed Maginess smirk. "Quite frankly," he continued, "I'd be lying if I said I was confident you were up to it."

"I tend to agree with you, Captain." It was Maginnes.

"You pipe down," Hill turned on the private investigator. "From what I can see you haven't exactly earned investigator of the year honors."

"Cap," Murphy decided it was his turn, "I understand your concerns, I really do, but I got this. I'll find Lyndsay." He said it because he believed it. "And right now I don't need help, especially his," he pointed at Maginnes. "Who is this guy anyway?"

"He is who and what he says he is," the Captain was calmer. "A P.I. named Johnny Maginnes."

"Who hired him?"

"I was hired," Maginnes answered instead of Hill, "to keep an eye on Lyndsay Howlund and I'm here because she's missing."

"Didn't do a very good job on that whole 'keeping an eye on' thing did you?"

"Detective, that's enough." It was Hill.

"I'm afraid you're right Detective Murphy," Maginnes added.

"You done?" The Captain asked Murphy.

"Yes sir."

"I'm working for Miss Howlund's mother," Maginnes picked up his story, "She was worried about her little girl traveling all over the world with a rock and roll band."

"Turns out she had good reason to be worried," Captain Hill added.

"We don't know that yet," Murphy offered, "She may have just needed some alone time."

"I appreciate you trying to be optimistic," Hill spoke like the girl's uncle, not the detective's superior.

"If she was so worried," Murphy addressed the private eye, "Why did she let her leave New Hampshire?"

"New Hampshire?" Maginnes looked puzzled.

"Yeah, New London," Murphy answered, "That's where she said she grew up."

"She lied," Maginnes and Hill said at the same time.

"What? Why?"

"Beats me," the P.I. answered.

"She's from Southern California," the Captain chimed in. "Her Mom, my sister, Chloe Hill is a pretty well-known casting director in Hollywood.

Lyndsay's a 'valley girl'," he said, referring to the San Fernando valley near Los Angeles.

"She sounded so convincing," Murphy lamented.

"Part of her talent," Maginnes said, "And her charm."

"But why would she lie?"

"Why wouldn't she? Look, it's a complicated relationship," the Captain explained. "They really didn't see eye to eye on a lot of things. Chloe wanted Lyndsay to plan ahead for her future..." Murphy looked at Maginnes who sat, nonplussed. The Captain continued, "Lyndsay was much more of a carpe diem kinda girl. Sis thought she should go to an Ivy League school, at least Duke or Vanderbilt; be a lawyer or a doctor. But since the time the girl was ten or so, she had dreams of Julliard." Murphy could tell his Captain was speaking from the heart and it made him wonder if all the previous redundancies weren't specifically aimed at him. Then he remembered the sniggers and the smirks and the laughter and changed his mind. "Lyndsay was much more like Chloe's husband's brother, Laurence."

"Laurence?" Maginnes asked.

"Laurence Howlund, Lyndsay's uncle on her father's side. He was much less buttoned down than my sister. He was footloose, impulsive. Lyndsay always thought he was a lot of fun. Ever since she was a little baby," Murphy thought the Captain sounded envious and silly. "He's an actor, goes by Laurence Matthews."

"Speaking of Lyndsay's father," Murphy had a question, "Where is he? How does he fit into this puzzle?"

"He doesn't," Hill answered quickly. "He and my sis went their separate ways when Lyndsay was little. Nobody on this side of the family has seen or heard from him since. Quite frankly, nobody wanted to."

"What about Laurence or Lyndsay?"

"No idea."

"But she uses his last name?" Murphy thought that was odd.

"Worth asking about," It was Maginnes. Captain Hill shrugged.

"You mentioned Orlando earlier," Hill turned to the detective, "What's there?"

"A guy from the band's road crew, actually a guitar tech. Joined the band right before the things started to go missing."

"Why didn't you rattle his chain here?" Maginnes wondered.

"He's missing too."

"No kidding?"

"Orlando was where he was working and living before he joined Serious Crisis on the road."

"Okay, good," Hill indicated the meeting was coming to an end, "You head to Florida. But Murphy?"

"Sir?"

"If you don't come up with something solidly concrete soon I'm bringing in Vance Veezy from Missing Persons because I'm going to do whatever it takes to find my niece."

"Understood," Murphy said, "I am too."

"And what about you?" he asked Maginnes.

"I'm going back to LA."

On his way home Murphy returned Mal Turner's call. He learned Marty Kaufmann was still in the Orlando system. He maintained his Florida driver's license and according to Turner still had a Central Florida address. Murphy thanked his friend and told him he'd be in Orlando soon. Turner requested Murphy check in with him when he arrived and the detective promised to do just that. It was cop courtesy, plus Murphy knew it would be good to see his old pal. They said goodbye and Murphy immediately called Charlie Carlucci.

"Hello, this is Charlie."

"Charlie, hi. It's Murphy Murphy. Would you do me the honor of joining me for dinner?" He got right to the point but was afraid the sentence included one too many "me's".

"Why I'd love to." She didn't seem to care about the me factor, "I was afraid you had forgotten about me."

"Impossible," Murphy answered honestly, "Pick you up at eight?"

"Perfect."

Keith Hirshland

MURPHY MURPHY ADDS AN ADDITIONAL TRIP TO HIS SCHEDULE

Murphy's flight to Orlando was uneventful except for the handful of screaming, crying, kicking toddlers who were headed to see princesses, pirates, and Harry Potter. The central Florida city had been home to Walt Disney World since 1971 and Universal Studios came nineteen years later. It welcomed millions of tourists every month and if the airplane Murphy rode was any indicator, this month would be no different. As Murphy heard a mother chastise her child another time, he recalled the only thing worse than going to Orlando was leaving. Long airport lines of tired children and grouchy parents awaited him, but he'd deal with that when the time came. One, two days at the most. His first order of business was to track down any residual evidence of rock 'n roll roadie and guitar tuner Marty Kaufmann. He called Mal Turner from his taxicab.

"Welcome to O-town detective. I trust your travels were comfortable."

"Smooth sailing," Murphy told a little white lie.

"I've got the information you requested," Turner said, "I'm about to grab a bite to eat, care to join me?" At the mention of food Murphy realized he hadn't eaten since breakfast with Charlie.

"Sounds good. Where?"

"Outback on Kirkman." Turner gave him the address and Murphy relayed the change of plans to his driver.

"Be there in ten," Murphy hung up.

The detectives exchanged greetings, caught up, shared stories over a "Bloomin' Onion" and had an early dinner. Turner offered to hang on to Murphy's overnight bag while the detective went in search of clues about Marty Kaufmann.

"Gives me an excuse to see you later and find out what you find out."

By the time Murphy left the restaurant with a full belly and the last known address for Marty Kaufmann, dusk was transitioning into a beautiful central Florida evening. The address was for an apartment in an 1800-acre master planned community that, since opening to great fanfare thirty years ago, had fallen into various states of disrepair. Half a million-dollar homes shared real estate with one and two bedroom rentals. Some areas were nice, others not so much. The car pulled up to a building that could be categorized as the latter. Murphy thanked the driver, got out and headed up a flight of stairs. His navy sport coat concealed his gun, holstered on his hip, and his shield, clipped to his belt. He hoped he wouldn't need either. It took only a minute to find Kaufmann's unit. He knocked.

"Mr. Kaufmann?" he knocked a little louder, "Marty Kaufmann? It's the police, open up please."

"You lookin to get shot at?" a male voice called from the floor above.

"I'd like to avoid that," Murphy answered, "Like you should avoid ending a sentence with a preposition."

"Oh, okay," the voice said, "You lookin to get shot at, Jerk?"

"Better," Murphy acknowledged, "Why would someone shoot at me?"

"No reason," the man laughed. "Banging on doors in the dark, announcing you're the police. Absolutely right, can't think of why a strange cop might attract a certain kind of attention in this neck of the woods. Besides, dude's not there, left months ago."

"Anybody else move in?"

"Nope. Empty."

Murphy looked around. He noticed the area in front of Kaufmann's door was debris free. No mess, no dried leaves, no mail, newspapers, or magazines.

"Where's the junk mail? The magazines?" he asked.

"No idea."

"Really?"

"Alright, I guess I might have an idea."

"Do tell."

"Lady in 302. Look, it's none of my business but it wasn't a hidden secret that the two of them were tight."

"Thanks for that."

"Be careful out there."

"Hill Street Blues fan?" Murphy asked.

"Desk Sergeant Paul Esterhaus," the voice said just before Murphy heard a door slide closed. Seconds later Murphy knocked on the door marked 302.

"Who is it?" a female voice responded from the other side.

"Police, ma'am. Please open the door."

"I haven't done anything wrong. Not so much as a parking ticket."

"Didn't say you had ma'am. I'd just like to ask you a few questions."

"Who do you think you are Alex Trebek? Questions about what?"

178

"Very funny," Murphy said, because he thought it was. "Questions about Marty Kaufmann."

"Show me your badge," the woman said, "Can't be too trusting around here." Murphy pulled his shield from his belt and held it up to the peep hole in the door. The next thing he heard was the chain lock slide and then the door opened a crack. "What happened to Marty?"

"Unclear if anything happened to him. He may be missing."

"May be?"

"Can I please come in ma'am?" After about ten seconds the door opened wider and the woman stood aside. Murphy walked into the entryway. With one sweep of his eyes he noticed a fair sized living area, a small kitchen, and an even smaller dining area. *Open concept* Murphy thought, *perfect for entertaining*. There was a small pile of mail on the dining room table and in one corner of the living room he noticed a mahogany Fender acoustic guitar and a Titleist golf bag filled with clubs.

"Getting a good look?" the woman, clad in a long house dress and slippers, said. Murphy's mother would have called it a muumuu.

"I'm sorry, ma'am, I'm detective Murphy. Thank you for agreeing to speak with me."

"Bev Beverly," the woman extended her right hand.

179

"Beverly Beverly?" Murphy took it and shook.

"Don't start," she warned

"Wouldn't dream of it," Murphy Murphy empathized. "Those your golf clubs?" he pointed. "All that mail belong to you?"

"Excuse me detective but is all this about me or Marty?"

"Maybe both," Murphy answered, "How well did you know him Mrs. Beverly?"

"Miss," she corrected him, "And I'm not sure the extent of my relationship with Mr. Kaufmann is any of your concern." Murphy studied the woman. He guessed she was in her mid to late 60's, graying, dirty blonde hair, brown eyes. She was about six inches shorter than he was which put her, in Murphy's estimation, at five feet five inches tall. Her weight was nearly impossible to tell under the full-length frock, but neither her face not her arms appeared to carry a lot of extra skin.

"My apologies again, ma'am. Just that the fellow above Mr. Kaufmann's apartment intimated that the two of you were close." Beverly Beverly snorted.

"This world would be a much better place if certain people learned to mind their own business."

"Yes ma'am."

180

"Marty and I were colleagues. I was the receptionist slash office manager for a magazine when he started working there too."

"Golf magazine?"

"Oh goodness no," she chuckled, "A local rag called *Orlando Today*. Stories and pictures about all the fun things folks could do in The City Beautiful." She used her fingers to illustrate quotation marks around the last three words. "He left after a little more than a year, hired away by *Golfer's Weekly*. I stayed until OT folded," she lamented, "but Marty and I remained good friends. I always thought he was a talented writer. He was quite a good guitar player too," she added.

"So those," Murphy looked toward the golf clubs and the guitar, "aren't yours?"

"Heavens no," she shook her head, "They belong to Marty. He asked me to keep them safe while he was gone."

"Mind if I take a look inside the golf bag?" Murphy asked, thinking the pockets would easily hold the items gone missing from Serious Crisis.

"Do you have a warrant?" she asked. Murphy was taken aback.

"I could certainly get one…" he started.

"I'm just pulling your leg detective," she smiled, "I always wanted to say that."

"Good to have goals," Murphy deadpanned as he pulled a pair of latex gloves from his back pocket and slipped them on. Before heading over to the golf bag Murphy looked again at the mail on the table, "That Marty's too?"

"Some of it's his, some mine. He asked me to check it and forward anything that looked important."

"Forward it where?" Murphy tried not to sound too excited.

"Different places in different cities," she answered. "He'd text me an address every few weeks."

"When was the last time you received one of those texts?"

"Oh, I don't know," she pulled her phone from a pocket, "A couple of weeks, I guess." She pressed some buttons and held the screen so the detective could see it. He saw a North Carolina address and Marty Kaufmann's telephone number. He forgot about one and memorized the other.

"Did he ever *send* mail here?"

"Never," she answered without thinking, "Outgoing only, no incoming."

Murphy walked over to the golf bag and started unzipping pockets. He found scorecards, pencils, a few coins, golf gloves, tees and balls. All of the white spheres were Titleists, and none of them had "Stray Dog" stamped on them. He also came across a sleeveless windbreaker from someplace called Seminole in another pocket. It shared space with what Murphy decided was some kind of distance measuring device from a company named Leupold. The detective put everything back where he found it, zipped up the pockets, and pulled off his gloves.

"Did Marty indicate when he might be coming back?"

"Never said when, just said he was."

Murphy pulled out one of his business cards and handed it to Beverly Beverly.

"If you think of anything else, or if you hear from Mr. Kaufmann again, please give me a call." The woman stared at the card and smiled. She didn't say a word. "I'll let myself out," Murphy said and he did.

On the way down the steps he pulled out his phone. First he recalled the numbers associated with Marty Kaufmann on Beverly Beverly's device and saved them and then he called Mal Turner.

"Finished so soon?" Turner said as soon as he answered.

"Yep," Murphy replied, "My work here is done, at least for now. Figured I'd swing by, grab my bag and head over to OIA."

"No flights to where you're headed tonight," Turner said with certainty.

"Guess I'll just get a room at the Hyatt there."

"I have a better idea. Why don't you stay here? Jess and Silver would love it." Murphy knew Jess was Mal's wife, Jessica, and Silver was Adam Silver, the couple's Australian shepherd. "Besides I've got an unopened bottle of Midleton Single Cask 1999 Pot Still Irish and I'm dying to hear what you found out."

"That's a four hundred dollar bottle of whiskey," Murphy was impressed, "You sure you want to waste some of it on me?"

"It was a gift."

"Well then, that's an offer I can't refuse," they both laughed. "You still on Calliope?" Murphy remembered the house from a previous trip.

"Same place," Turner confirmed.

"I'll call a cab, be there shortly."

"A cab?" Turner sounded surprised, "People still use cabs?"

"I do," Murphy said, not sure what the big deal was, "As opposed to what, hitchhike?"

"You're funny Murphy. I was thinking more like an Uber or a Lyft." There was silence on the other end. "You know, ridesharing companies? They're all the rage now. Cleaner, faster, cheaper." Murphy still had no response. "Nevermind, call your cab," Turner said and hung up.

The taxi arrived, Murphy sat back, closed his eyes and thought about the last half hour or so. Kaufmann had not been back to Orlando since joining Serious Crisis, at least not that Murphy could tell. But he also hadn't severed ties completely with Central Florida, Beverly Beverly assured him of that. He was still paying rent; a quick search of a real estate app showed the detective that nut was about $1,000 a month. Murphy made a mental note to ask Jeff Giucigiu how much a guitar tech makes. Kaufmann hadn't been completely truthful about leaving Orlando or about the extent or quality of his golf game. Murphy wondered why and whether it mattered. He also suspected there was more to the Kaufmann/Beverly Beverly relationship, but he needed more time and information to decide what that might be. He'd ask Mal Turner to do a little digging on the woman. He grabbed his phone and dialed Johnny "Jack" Maginnes to see if he had made any progress on his end, then he put in a call to Charlie Carlucci just to hear her voice. Both went to voicemail. He left a message for Charlie.

"Do you know the code?" the driver asked as they pulled up the gated community.

"Let me make a call," Murphy replied. At that instant the gate started to swing open. Murphy disconnected.

"Well what do you know," the driver said under his breath.

"It's up there on the left," Murphy said

Silver was indeed thrilled to see Murphy Murphy. He barked and jumped and presented the nearest toy to his new playmate. Jessica, Turner's wife, seemed less enthusiastic.

"Hello Murphy," she said giving him what felt to Murphy like an obligatory hug. "Nice to see you again." She walked over to her husband and kissed him on the forehead. "I'm going upstairs to read," He smiled and nodded. "I'm sure you two detectives have a lot to discuss." She kissed Mal again, this time on the lips. "There are clean towels in the bathroom Murphy, make yourself at home."

"Thank you, Jessica," Murphy smiled, "I won't keep your husband too long."

"Keep him as long as you need," she said turning to leave the room, "I'll get my fair share of him later."

"I'm counting on that!" Mal Turner said to her back.

Murphy held the crystal glass, half filled with amber liquid up to the light in Mal Turner's study. He put the jigger to his nose and was immediately surprised by and pleased with the bouquet. He sensed tropical varieties of fruit including kiwi, mango and banana. When he closed his eyes he thought he could also smell marshmallow and maybe even rosewater. He couldn't wait to taste it, so he didn't.

"Magnificent," he said admiringly.

"Glad you like it," Turner said as he took a sip of his own drink, a Pappy Van Winkle twenty three-year-old bourbon.

"Another *gift?*" Murphy asked referring to the Pappy. Turner shrugged.

"Is it my fault that I have a C.I. that appreciates the fact that I keep his identity a secret?" Murphy knew the term C.I. was in reference to a confidential informant. "What did you find over at Kaufmann's?" Turner changed the subject. Before answering Murphy looked around the study. He saw several pictures of his detective friend surrounded by, what must have been, dignitaries and sports stars. There was also a plaque or two celebrating Malachai J. Turner and his philanthropic efforts.

"He's gone, but not for good."

"How can you be sure?"

"Couple reasons," Murphy savored another sip of the whiskey. "Nosy neighbor would have said so, plus Kaufmann has a friend in the same complex. She forwards his mail, keeps an eye on his stuff."

"*She?*"

"Not like that," Murphy caught Turner's inference. "More like a big sister or an aunt."

"Does she have a key to his place?" Turner asked him a question Murphy realized he had failed to ask her.

"I didn't ask," Murphy admitted and took another sip of whiskey. "Captain Hill is thinking about bringing in more manpower, maybe Missing Persons. Not sure he has a ton of confidence in me at the moment."

"Don't be silly Murphy," Turner offered consolation, "I know you're a good cop and what's more you're a solid guy. Can't beat that combination." Murphy smiled an appreciative smile. "The key thing was a minor oversight. I'm not even sure I would have asked the question at the time. You want me to check her out? Do some digging?"

"Couldn't hurt."

"Name?"

"Beverly Beverly." With that Turner coughed up a little of his bourbon.

"No wonder you didn't go too hard at her," he toasted Murphy Murphy, "Kindred spirit."

"Maybe," Murphy said.

"Tell me more about this private investigator." Turner was on to the next thing.

"Johnny "Jack" Maginnes?" Murphy answered.

"Yeah. That guy. What's his story?"

"Former SEAL. Ex-cop, Dallas P.D., if memory serves me, and now a P.I."

"Funny," Mal said shaking his head.

"In what way?"

"It's been my experience that guys with that kind of pedigree go into contract work with big corporations or even the government. Either that or they end up on some cable tv network as an expert on this that and the other thing. Not too many become private dicks."

"This one did."

"Clearly," Turner nodded, "But why?"

"Not sure I'm following."

"Let me put it another way," Mal took a sip of bourbon. "It seems this guy should be in high demand, phone ringing off the hook. Not hanging around some rock band. Who hired him?"

"Girl's mother, Chloe Hill." Turner looked at the ceiling for a good ten seconds.

"Navy SEAL," he finally said, "Dallas P.D." he added, "And no red flags on when you ran the search?"

"None," Murphy leaned forward in his chair.

"This guy was well trained," Turner continued to think out loud, "had extensive law enforcement experience, and then leaves professional soldiering and policing to hang his own shingle."

"Pretty much sums it up."

"SEALS are the best of the best, right?"

"Right up there with Green Berets and Army Special Forces, sure," Murphy agreed.

"And the Dallas police department has a good reputation," Turner continued.

"For a city that size, one of the best," Murphy agreed again. "Where are you going with this?"

"So, if all of that is true you'd think Johnny "Jack" Maginnes would be a pretty decent investigator, right?"

"I'd think so."

"Then how does he lose track of a twenty-something female rock star he's presumably being paid good money not to lose track of?"

"That, Malachai Turner," Murphy said after silently forgiving his friend for ending his sentence with a preposition, "is a darn good question."

Murphy fell asleep thinking about two questions; the one he didn't ask Beverly Beverly and the last one Mal Turner asked him. Whether exhausted or affected by the whiskey, Murphy slept like a dead guy and dreamt uneasy dreams of dismal, dusty rooms and dirty cops, loud bangs and barely audible whispers. He snored through his alarm and only woke up because Silver was expending a great deal of effort licking his face. A sluggish look at his phone told Murphy he still had time to make his flight, if just barely, and he had missed two phone calls. One was from Serious Crisis manager, Jeff Giucigiu. The other from an 818 area code that Murphy didn't recognize.

As it turned out he got to the airport, and then the gate, in plenty of time. A detective's shield did wonders at crowded security lines. He grabbed a cup of chain store tea and sat down in one of the uncomfortable chairs designed so people wouldn't, or couldn't, sleep in them. He called Jeff Giucigiu back.

"This is Jeff."

"Mr. Giucigiu, it's Detective Murphy. You called?"

"I did sir. Thank you for calling me back. We found Marty Kaufmann."

"Did we? Where?"

"Mother of Eternal Mercy Hospital," he answered. Murphy knew the place well. "He's been there for the last three nights."

"What happened?"

"Doc said it was an allergic reaction," Giucigiu said, "Bad sushi."

"That's redundant," Murphy offered an opinion, "Have you seen him?"

"Last night, just before I called you. The reaction was still visible to the eye."

'That's also redundant."

"Pardon?" the manager sounded confused.

"Never mind," Murphy shook his head, "Call the hospital back and tell them not to discharge Mr. Kaufmann until I have had a chance to speak with him. Please."

"Okay," Giucigiu responded. "But when will that be? Where are you?"

"Just tell them Jeff." Murphy disconnected and tossed his phone onto the seat beside him. He couldn't believe this case. Something seemed solid one minute then it turned to mush the next. A lead had legs and then suddenly it drifted away like smoke. Murphy Murphy had Kaufmann penciled in as a prime candidate for the past forty hours only to have that erased because the guy had spent that time in a hospital bed. *He did eat sushi*, Murphy thought, *so I guess it serves him right*. Then there was Mags, who had gone from a person of interest to part of the team and back to being suspicious. It seemed to Murphy that every time he caught a break his hopes were shattered. His phone buzzed.

"Murphy."

"Detective, it's Jeff again."

"Go ahead."

"I called the hospital and they said not to worry, Marty isn't going anywhere until at least tomorrow."

"Thank goodness," Murphy let out a breath.

"Excuse me, detective? That's terrible news," the manager chastised.

"For you maybe," Murphy replied, "for Kaufmann certainly," he added. "But not for me."

"Goodbye detective." Giucigiu clicked off. Murphy got on the plane.

Back home Murphy went straight to the hospital. After ignoring him for the requisite amount of time and searching her computer for an additional, aggravating, few minutes, the nurse at the desk told him Marty Kaufmann was in room 2323. The detective headed up the stairs and down the hall. Murphy found the man in bed, eyes closed, head propped up by pillows. His face was red and still swollen. Some game show was on the TV.

"Mr. Kaufmann?" Murphy entered the room, "You awake?"

"Can't sleep" came out as "Kahhhnn Sthlee" thanks, Murphy deduced, to a swollen tongue. Kaufmann opened his eyes.

"How are you feeling?" Murphy asked what he knew was a stupid question. Marty just shrugged his shoulders. "If you're up for it," the detective continued, "I'd like to ask you some questions about the other night."

"Aaathhk."

"What happened?"

"Baaahh Uhhnnee."

"Sorry?" Murphy leaned in.

"Bad uni," a female voice behind Murphy chimed in. A nurse, or a doctor, Murphy wasn't sure, had joined them. He turned around and saw a young woman in scrubs holding a clipboard. "I'm Doctor Kelly," she said, "Kelly Kelly."

"Of course you are," Murphy replied. "What's bad uni?"

"Sea urchin gonads," she answered.

"Excuse me?"

"Sushi. You know, raw fish?" she elaborated, "People eat it."

"I don't." Murphy shook his head.

"Then you don't know what you're missing," the doctor responded, "It's delicious."

"Sea urchin gonads are delicious?" Murphy couldn't or wouldn't believe it.

"Sure," she exclaimed, "if prepared correctly. So is octopus, salmon skin, giant clam, and even fugu."

"Fugu?"

"Pufferfish," she closed her eyes, "Exquisite."

"That may be," the detective conceded, "but I'm never going to end up like this guy," Murphy pointed at Kaufmann, "by eating a nice, thick, New York strip steak."

"I wouldn't be so sure," the doctor warned.

"I'll take my chances," Murphy decided. "So, Mr. Kaufmann here ate some bad sea urchin gonads?" he asked.

"Before I answer your question, do you mind if I ask you one?"

"Shoot."

"Who are you and what do you want with my patient?"

"That's two questions," Murphy said as he pulled his coat back revealing his detective's shield. "I'm Detective Murphy and I need to ask your patient some questions. The doctor considered Murphy Murphy for a long moment.

"Beside eating uni at a second-rate sushi restaurant, is my patient suspected of being guilty of something?" That made Murphy smile.

"Because of his current condition I would say that's highly doubtful," he answered, "but he may provide information about an ongoing investigation."

"Fair enough," she said setting the clipboard down and shoving her hands into the pockets of her scrubs. "What do you want to know?"

"When was Mr. Kaufmann admitted?" The question forced Doctor Kelly to refer back to the clipboard.

"Give me a brief moment," she said as much to herself as Murphy, "Looks like three nights ago, just before one am."

"Do you mind if I ask where you went to school?"

"UNC Chapel Hill for undergrad," she said proudly, "Then Hopkins. Why?"

"Just curious. So, he was admitted between midnight and one am three days ago? Suffering from an allergic reaction? And he's still here. Is that normal?"

"I've found there is rarely a "normal" in medicine detective, but you're correct. Under different circumstances Mr. Kaufmann would have been treated and released within twenty four hours."

"What, exactly, were Marty's, uh Mr. Kaufmann's, circumstances?"

"It seems we treated him with a steroid that caused an additional allergic reaction."

"It seems?"

"We did."

"So, he was allergic to the sushi and then while treating that, you made things worse."

"We did," she repeated the admission. Murphy looked over at Kaufmann who had been listening the entire time. For the second time that morning, he shrugged.

"The good news is," the doctor continued, "we now have it under control and Mr. Kaufmann should be able to get out of here sometime today."

"Dahht isth guu newth," Kaufmann said.

"Thanks doc. I just need another few minutes with Marty."

"No worries," she smiled, "Just don't stay too long. I can't predict in advance how he might react." Murphy nodded.

"Did they not teach English at those citadels of higher education?" he said as the door closed behind her.

It took more than half an hour, between Marty's swollen tongue, multiple sips of water and one intrusive nurse, but Murphy got his answers. Marty Kaufmann confirmed that he had, indeed, gone to a late night sushi restaurant alone after the show. He'd eaten tuna, salmon, octopus, and something he called a rainbow roll. Then, for reasons known only to Kaufmann, Murphy learned Marty decided what he needed to complete the meal was a piece of uni. According to the patient the reaction was close to immediate. He told the detective he knew right away he was in an "emergency situation". Murphy let that one go and encouraged Kaufmann to continue. Marty said he called 911 from his phone and waited ten to fifteen minutes for paramedics to arrive. He added, in disgust, while he waited, struggling for breath, the waitress brought over the check for him to sign. Murphy took notes, knowing most if not all of Kaufmann's story could be corroborated. During the conversation Murphy thought he could see Marty's condition improving. He was happy about that.

"I just have a couple more questions if you're up for it," Murphy had said after remembering what his friend Judith Colman had told him.

"Mnahh gonn anywahh," Kaufmann had said, pointing to the tubes going in and out of his arm.

"Did you get into it with Lyndsay Howlund during the show?" Murphy asked and Kaufmann responded with a quizzical look. "During the concert the other night, did you and Miss Howlund have a disagreement?" Murphy noticed it looked like a light had gone on behind Marty's eyes. From his bed, he nodded. "What about?" Murphy asked.

"Whhong thhrings," a fat tongue spat out.

"Wrong strings?" Murphy asked for confirmation. Kaufmann nodded again.

"Ahh usethed thuh whhong whon on hurr gitthar."

"The Martin?"

"Uhhh huhh. Muhh Muhh ungeed," Kaufmann added.

"Mo Mo thought something was wrong? Something was off?" Murphy wanted to make sure he had that right. "And Lyndsay got angry." Kaufmann nodded another time.

"Ah thhukewed uhp, und thee wuth cuhwekt." This time Kaufmann shrugged shoulders.

"When was the last time you saw her, Marty?" Kaufmann appeared to think for a moment before responding.

"Whin thee wawk awwff snaje."

Murphy understood. Marty Kaufmann had nothing to do with the disappearance of either Lyndsay Howlund or her acoustic guitar.

"Feel better," he said, tapping the patient on the leg. Kaufmann closed his eyes.

On the way out Murphy figured he better call Mal Turner and give him an update on Kaufmann.

"Detective Murphy," Turner said answering his phone, "what a co inky dink. I was just about to give you a call. I trust you made it home okay."

"Safe and sound," Murphy responded, "Why were you going to call me?"

"You first."

"Okay. I was calling to thank you again for the hospitality and to tell you the Marty Kauffman matter is no longer an issue. Now you."

"Anytime," Turner responded to the first part, "and maybe the matter is no longer an issue for you," was his answer to the second.

"What do you mean?"

"Well, after our chat last night I sent an email to my team requesting they start the day doing some digging on your girl Beverly Beverly."

"And?" Murphy asked, interested.

"And… it turns out that's not her real name."

"I knew it!" Murphy exclaimed. "You know what they say, never trust a person with two first names." They both laughed.

"Turns out Bev Beverly was just one of many aliases for one Candace Candiotti. She's got quite a sheet."

"Candy Candiotti?" Murphy laughed again.

"I know, right?" Anyway, she was Cathy Crowder when she worked at Orlando Today. Seems she wasn't thrilled with the take home pay and decided to pocket a little extra on the side."

"Embezzlement?" Murphy asked.

"Exactly. Did eighteen months over in Hernando then had to pay it all back. That was enough for us to go to a judge and get a warrant to search her place."

"Because of Kauffman? That seems like a bit of a leap."

"Would be if it was only because of Kauffman, but there's been an uptick of porch piracy in that part of town."

"Pirates stealing porches?"

"Very funny Murphy, but no. Somebody, or somebodies, stealing package deliveries right off people's porches or decks. It's a thing here these days."

"Man, people suck," was all Murphy could think to say.

"Some sure do, my friend," Turner concurred, "some sure do."

"What happened?"

"We got the warrant and headed her way. Found dozens of packages, none of them addressed to her, in the garage. Looks like Kauffman is going to have to find another place to store his golf clubs and guitar."

"Not to mention finding another way to get his mail," Murphy added.

"Speaking of Kauffman, what's his deal? Why is he off the hook?"

"He's been in the hospital for three days. Bad sushi."

"That sounds awful."

"You have no idea."

"Thanks for the update," Turner said sounding ready to go, "Sorry this means a step back or two in your investigation."

"Way it goes," Murphy said, "Still a couple of other leads to track down." He was thinking of Maginnes.

"Good luck. Stay safe."

"You too." They both hung up. Murphy saw Dr. Kelly Kelly coming his way.

"I just signed Kaufmann's discharge papers," she said smiling, "He can go home today."

"He'll be happy to hear that," Murphy replied. "By the way, is Kelly Kelly your real name?" he asked thinking about Cathy Crowder/Candy Candiotti/Beverly Beverly. The doctor smiled like she'd heard the question a million times.

"Since the day Doctor Pascutti smacked me on the behind."

"Thanks doc."

"Have a good day detective." They went their separate ways and Murphy's phone rang. He noticed the number was coming from police headquarters.

"Murphy," he answered.

"Is there a reason you're not returning my sister's phone calls?" It was Captain Hill.

"No sir," he said honestly, "quite frankly I didn't know she called."

"Check for an 818 number," the Captain said and he hung up before Murphy could assure him he would.

"Hello," Chloe Hill answered

"Ms. Hill?" Murphy asked

"Speaking," she replied, "Who's calling?" she asked although Murphy suspected she knew exactly who was calling. He thought her voice sounded like a hive of bees; distressed, persistent, exhausted, but at the same time completely in control.

"This is detective Murphy Murphy. I apologize for taking so long to return your call, ma'am."

"Well it's about time," she scolded, "and for goodness sake don't call me ma'am. It makes me sound so old."

"Yes ma'am," Murphy said on purpose.

"Have you located my daughter?" she asked, adding anger to the emotions Murphy was sure he heard.

"Not yet," he answered honestly. "I assume Mr. Maginnes has filled you in on our investigation."

"You know what happens when you assume, don't you detective?" she asked. Murphy knew. "You make an ass out of you and me," she told him anyway. "To assume I have spoken to Mr. Maginnes about my daughter's disappearance would do just that." The comment took Murphy by surprise.

"I just thought the investigator who works for you might have brought you up to speed on where the case stands at this time."

"Mr. Maginnes no longer works for me."

"Since when?"

"Since I fired him," Chloe Hill stated the obvious.

"And when did you do that, ma'am?" Murphy didn't even try to mask his annoyance.

"I don't know exactly," she seemed to stop and think for a moment, "maybe three weeks ago. Could have been a month."

"Did you happen to mention this fact to your brother, Captain Hill?"

"I didn't happen to mention it to anyone."

"And why, exactly, did you terminate his services?"

"Because continuing to pay him was, quite simply, a waste   of   my   money."

"In what way?" Murphy was genuinely curious.

"In so many ways," as she said this Murphy thought her tone turned pensive. "Do you have any children, detective?"

"I do not," was Murphy's only response.

"I realize legally my daughter is a grown woman but, at times, she still seems like such a little girl. She can take care of herself, lord knows she told me that a million times, but a mother can't help but worry, can she?" This time Murphy didn't respond. "I mean a rock and roll band full of testosterone raging boys," Murphy could have sworn he heard her shaking her head, "not to mention the lifestyle."

"Ma'am?" Murphy asked not knowing what she meant.

"Oh please! I'm no prude but I do work in Hollywood. The drugs, the drinking, the late nights, the hangers-on, they're everywhere."

"So, that's why you hired someone to spy on your daughter? Because you assumed the worst?" Murphy asked, although he suspected he was crossing a line.

"Don't judge me," she confirmed his suspicions, "don't you dare."

"My sincere apologies, Ms. Hill," Murphy offered, thinking about his Captain's wrath, "I was out of line."

"Yes you were," she let that sink in for a moment. "Anyway, it didn't matter what my motivation for hiring Mr. Maginnes was, every report was the same. Different cities, for sure, but similar details. No drama, nothing illegal, just life on the road with a rock band. Mr. Maginnes painted a picture of a young woman on a Girl Scout expedition. I determined either nothing untoward was going on or my private investigator was lying to me. Either way my money was being wasted. Now if you'll excuse me I have a casting call," she said, clearly finished with Murphy Murphy.

"Just one more question, if you don't mind?" he asked.

"I do mind but go ahead," she sighed.

"Why would Lyndsay tell me she grew up in New Hampshire?" Murphy asked, recalling his conversation with Lyndsay.

"Larry," she said without thinking.

"I'm sorry. Do you mean Laurence your brother in law?"

"One and the same," she said, "Lyndsay's uncle. He's an actor," she added.

"Right," Murphy remembered, "so I've been told. But what does he have to do with my question?"

"The man's whole world is make believe, always has been, detective. And he did everything he could to make sure Lyndsay's was too. He would constantly engage her in what they both called the 'what if' game."

"The 'what if' game?" Murphy wondered
"Larry maintained it was an activity that sparked her imagination. What if you could fly? What if you could talk to animals? What if you lived in the woods of some faraway place like Maine or New Hampshire? Lyndsay couldn't get enough of it, it drove me absolutely crazy."

"You didn't appreciate him teaching her to play make believe?"

"I didn't appreciate anyone teaching her to waste her time. Life is hard, detective, it's not a place for flights of fancy." Murphy suddenly felt sorry for the woman and not just because her daughter was missing.

"He clearly had a profound effect on her when she was young," he offered.

"She loved him," she said, as Murphy thought he detected a hint of jealousy, "Still does."

"Have you spoken to your brother-in-law since Lyndsay went missing?"

"I thought you wanted to ask one more question," she said reminding him. "I haven't spoken to him in years," she answered anyway, "but not because I haven't tried. He simply refuses to return my calls."

"One more question," Murphy promised, "When was the last time you tried?" he asked before she could refuse.

"This morning," she sounded sad. "Find her for me detective, please. Just find her."

"I'm working on it, ma'am," this time saying it with respect. He hung up thinking he had another place he needed to look and a couple of people with whom he needed to speak. He dialed the precinct number, identified himself and then asked to be put through to the Captain's office. Marcia answered.

"Hi Marcia, it's Murphy Murphy. Is the Cap available?"
"Captain Hill is in his office," she sounded cross which, Murphy thought, was normal.

"May I speak with him?"

"Hold please," and she was gone.

"What is it detective?" the Captain asked. Murphy thought Marcia's grumpiness was rubbing off on his boss.

"I just spoke with your sister."
"Thank you for that."

"She told me one Johnny "Jack" Maginnes is no longer in her employ."

"What?" the Captain was genuinely surprised, "Since when?"

"Maybe a month," Murphy answered, "She wasn't exactly sure."

"You're kidding! But we all just met with each other a few days ago."

"Yes sir, we did," Murphy said exasperated.

"And he had already been fired? That's almost too incredible to believe." Murphy listened, speechless. "So, what now?"

"Your sister mentioned her actor brother-in-law. I thought I might make a run at him," Murphy said, knowing he was already heading west.

"Out in California?"

"That's correct."

"OK, I guess that makes a certain amount of sense. Last I heard he lived in the Hollywood Hills. But detective?"

"Captain," he said, making a mental note of the town.

"Fly coach and don't stay out there too long. The department of redundancy department's budget is dwindling down."

"Roger that," Murphy ended the call. "As opposed to dwindling up," he said to no one in particular. He knew he had to pack and wanted to call two of the people he cared most about. Judith didn't answer so he left a message, Charlie picked up on the first ring.

"Hello handsome."

"Miss Carlucci," he said blushing

"What can I do for you?" she asked

"Not a thing right this moment," he answered, "I just wanted to let you know that I have to go out of town again."

"The Serious Crisis Case?"

"Indeed."

"Where to this time good sir?"

"Los Angeles," he replied, "Gonna try to run down a movie star."

"Ooh really?" she sounded excited, "Which one? Brad Pitt? Tom Cruise? Chris Hemsworth?"

"None of the above," he said hoping not to disappoint her, "Laurance Matthews."

"Who?"

"Exactly. Anyway, I won't be away long but I'll miss you terribly when I'm gone."

"Aren't you sweet," she said sincerely. "Good luck, be careful, and come back home as fast as you can." "That's a 10-4," he answered.

"I just love it when you talk cop."

Murphy told her he'd check in when he got there, then hung up and headed home. The goal was to be in Southern California for as few days as possible and to accomplish that he'd need a plan and some help. Help, he figured, might come from several sources including Lyndsay Howlund's mother, Chloe Hill.

Murphy Murphy Heads to California with the Hope of Entirely Eliminating Some Suspects

Murphy Murphy looked out the window from his seat in the 22nd row. Los Angeles sprawled out below as the plane made its final approach into the Los Angeles International airport. Murphy instinctively started singing the 1969 Arlo Guthrie tune, "Coming into Los Angeles".

"Bringin in a couple of keys." His father, Murphy Murphy sang it every time they visited the city of angels, which turned out to be fairly regularly when Murphy was a kid. His grandparents lived, for a time, in the toney Palos Verdes Estates. A family visit always started with a recitation of the Guthrie song and almost always included a trip to Disneyland, Knotts Berry Farm or Marineland of the Pacific. Murphy loved Marineland the best. He could still recall how excited he felt watching the killer whales, Orky and Corky, perform. He wasn't yet ten when the owners of Sea World, further south near San Diego, bought the park then shuttered its doors and moved all the animals out. The neighborhood know-it-all, Stevie Sallery, told Murphy and his sister Muffy that the new owners put all the marine life in special trucks and transported them in the middle of the night. He added that they changed Corky's name to Shamu. All the kids agreed the new name was "weird and stupid" and pinky swore that Corky would always be Corky to them.

"Don't touch my bags if you please, Mister Customs Man." Murphy sang as the plane touched down. Chloe Hill had agreed to carve out a few minutes for Murphy, though only if they would meet at a Starbucks on San Vicente Boulevard in Brentwood. According to the GPS on his phone it should take about a half an hour to get there once he picked up his rental car. He found a shorter than expected line and approached the young man at the counter. The name tag on his chest indicated Murphy would be dealing with "Wes".

"Hello Wes," Murphy said, reaching into his pocket for his driver's license and a credit card. "I have a reservation. The name is Murphy."

"Yes sir," Wes responded pounding on a few computer keys. "How was your flight Mr. Murphy?"

"Fine," Murphy answered, even though he couldn't imagine Wes really cared.

"That's great," Wes said robotically, "Let's see," he tapped a couple more keys, "It looks like we have a pickup truck available." He looked at Murphy proudly.

"As opposed to another kind of truck?" Murphy asked

"What?" a clearly confused Wes wondered.

"Or a pickup car?"

"I'm sorry, you lost me," Wes admitted.

"I'm not surprised."

"So, do you want the pickup truck?"

"No I don't want the pickup truck, Wes. Do you have a Renault Le Car available?"

"A what?"

"Never mind," Murphy shook his head, "Just put me in whichever car pops up next."

Yes, sir," Wes went back to his keyboard, "How does a Chevy Malibu sound?"

"It sounds marvelous," Murphy said and he waited for a relieved Wes to give him the contract and the keys.

It took a little longer to get to Brentwood than the GPS indicated but Murphy was pleasantly surprised that the five lanes of north bound traffic on the 405 moved relatively smoothly. He exited at Wilshire and headed west toward his destination. He parked, fed the meter, and went inside where Chloe Hill was already waiting. She wasn't hard to recognize because Murphy thought she looked like a smaller, slightly prettier, version of her older brother.

"Thanks for agreeing to meet me, Ms. Hill," Murphy said as he pulled up a chair.

"The clock is ticking detective," she said looking at her watch. "I have to be out of here within the next fifteen minutes. The traffic on Wilshire this time of day can be brutal." Murphy tried to decide if she was being disagreeable or self-important. He decided it was probably a combination of both.

"Then I'll be brief. Do you have the information I requested?" Murphy had asked for the last known phone numbers and addresses for her brother-in-law and her former private investigator.

"I do," she said pulling a sheet of paper from her handbag. "But if you want my personal opinion, I'm not sure any of it will do you any good." Murphy wondered if redundancy was a family trait.

"Thank you," he took the paper. "Where is Woodrow Wilson Drive?" he asked after glancing at the information.

"In the hills," she answered, referring to the star-studded Hollywood Hills.

"Nice," he said with admiration, "There are some beautiful places up there."

"Larry has done okay for himself," she said in response.

"Has Lyndsay been to this house?" Murphy asked as Chloe sipped her tea, thinking.

"Certainly as a little girl," she answered, "Quite frankly I wouldn't know about a more recent period of time."

"If I may ask…"

"You may not," Chloe interjected before Murphy could ask his question. "Now if you'll excuse me, I'll be on my way." She gathered her belongings and stood. Being a gentleman Murphy stood too. "You owe Jayce behind the register five dollars."

"Jace?" Murphy asked.

"J-A-Y-C-E," she spelled it out, "the young lady at the counter," she pointed. "She poured me my tea." Then she showed Murphy her back and headed out of the coffee shop. Murphy watched her approach a Jaguar SUV, saw her stop, shake her head, and pull a parking ticket out from under the windshield wiper. She looked up and down San Vicente before stuffing the ticket into her purse. Then she got in the car and drove away. Murphy wanted not to like Chloe Hill, but he knew he'd be better served by cutting her some slack. He thought of the words uttered by his favorite comedian, Steve Martin, who said, "Before you criticize a man, walk a mile in his shoes. That way when you do criticize him, you'll be a mile away and have his shoes." Murphy chuckled to himself, paid Jayce for the tea, and dialed the number for Laurence Howlund, aka Laurence Matthews. It went straight to voicemail and a computer voice invited Murphy to leave a message, so he did.

Then he left the restaurant and climbed into his rental car, happy he had made the decision to put plenty of money in the parking meter. He punched the address Chloe Hill had given him for her brother-in-law into his phone and headed for the hills. Close to forty minutes later he took exit 14 off the 101 freeway then turned left on Mulholland and right on Woodrow Wilson. The house at the desired location was mostly hidden by trees and a large hedge. The entrance was guarded by a gate which Murphy wasn't surprised to find open. He pulled in and found, by Hollywood Hills standards, a modest house with a four-car garage. A white Jeep Grand Cherokee SRT was parked in front of the door farthest from the house.

A silver Aston Martin Vanquish was sitting majestically in the driveway perpendicular to the front door. Leaning on the left front fender was a man who, Murphy thought, looked vaguely familiar. He parked next to the Jeep, killed the engine, and got out of the car.

"You must be the detective who just left a message on my voicemail," the man said as Murphy approached.

"That's correct," Murphy answered, "I'm Detective Murphy Murphy, thank you for meeting me." Murphy pulled his coat back a little to show his shield. The actor said nothing as Murphy closed the distance between them. He held out his hand and the two shook. Laurence Matthews gave his visitor the once over and finally spoke.

"Buffalo buffalo buffalo Buffalo buffalo," he said, releasing Murphy's hand. Murphy Murphy had heard the words strung together before with as few as four "buffaloes" and as many as eight. An English teacher in middle school had introduced the grammatically correct, perfectly acceptable, sentence to the boy he considered his prized student. He assured the young Murphy that he meant no disrespect. He just thought it was a part of the English language that the pupil with the same first and last name should know. Murphy never forgot his explanation that it was an example of how homophones and homonyms could be used to create a complex linguistic construct. He smiled at the memory and the actor.

"Buffalo from the New York city of Buffalo bully other buffalo from Buffalo," Murphy said as he recited, word for word, the explanation of the sentence his teacher had given him decades before.

"I've always wanted to say that in a movie," Matthews said. "Why are you here detective?"

"Can we go inside?" Murphy asked as an answer.

"We can," the actor replied, "but we won't. Why are you here?" he asked again.

"Fine Mr. Matthews," Murphy acquiesced, "Or is it Mr. Howlund?"

"It's been both, at times. As well as a few others."

"You look familiar to me," Murphy said what he had thought earlier.

"I have appeared in dozens of television programs, several motion pictures and more commercials than I'd prefer to admit, so forgive me if I'm not surprised you find my mug familiar, detective. But I'll just take a wild guess and say you're not here for an autograph."

"Depends," Murphy said honestly making the actor smile. "When was the last time you saw your niece, Mr. Howlund?" Murphy asked as he watched the smile disappear. The detective wasn't sure what the sudden change in demeanor meant.

"Which one, detective? I have more than one," he offered information that was news to Murphy.

"Lyndsay, sir. Lyndsay Howlund." The mention of the name brought another, different smile.
"Sadly, it's been a while. I do enjoy that child's company. Why do you ask?"

"She's missing."

"Missing? From where? Since when?"

"She was last seen about a week ago after the rock band of which she's a member played a concert."

"Oh my God!" he exclaimed and Murphy tried to decide if the actor was acting. "That's disturbing."

"Yes, it is," Murphy agreed, "You haven't heard from her?"

"Not a peep," he answered quickly, "Certainly not within the last week. But if she does reach out I'll be sure to let you know." Murphy was having trouble shaking the feeling that the actor wasn't being one hundred percent truthful. "By the way," Howlund continued, "how did you get my number and address?"

"Your sister-in-law gave me what she had," Murphy replied. "Why are the two of you not on speaking terms?"

"What did she tell you?"

"She wouldn't give me a reason. Just said you won't return her calls."

"Old grudge," he said simply, "Past history." Murphy said nothing, hoping the actor was finished using redundant phrases but not finished talking. "A number of years ago my dear sister-in-law got a career break by being named the casting director for what turned out to be a very popular and financially lucrative movie." Murphy was glad the actor kept talking but he, of course, could have lived without the nonsense.

"Let me guess," he said, "you wanted her to give you a part."

"I didn't want her to *give* me a thing. I simply asked for the opportunity to read for a role. She denied me that even though we both knew I would have been perfect for the part. I was just starting out and it would have been an amazing launching pad for my career."

"What was her reason?" Murphy asked though he could guess.

"It was her first time working for a bigger name director and she said she didn't want to get a reputation around town as someone who supported nepotism."
"And you disagreed." It wasn't a question.

"I was furious. Truth be told I still am," he lamented, "I mean come on, *nepotism?* Good grief get a clue, this town was built on nepotism. It's still what sustains it. She was just being selfish," he shook his head.

"Who got the part?"

"Kid named Hanks. Heard of him?"

"I believe I have," Murphy sympathized and looked around at the surroundings. "But it appears you've done ok?"

"Can't complain," he agreed, "Except about my sister-in-law," he chuckled.

"Nice house in the Hollywood Hills, two amazing cars," he pointed first to the Aston Martin and then to the Jeep.

"Actually I have half a dozen automobiles," Howlund corrected him. "But that SRT isn't one of them." Murphy stared at the Jeep, then the building. "The garage is bigger than it looks," Howlund assured him, "Just like the house."

"Do you live here alone?" Murphy asked what he feared was too personal a question.

"I do. Always have. Why?"

"No reason," Murphy said knowing it was his turn to be less than truthful, "It's just that you implied that it's a big house. Must get lonely."

"I do okay," was his answer, "but thanks for your concern."

"My apologies," the detective was contrite, "I didn't mean to imply anything."

"Sure you did, detective," the actor countered, "but no harm no foul."

"So, who owns the Cherokee?" He got back to the Jeep.

"Friend of mine. Guy named Brian Katrek but I'm curious why that's any of your concern."

"Probably isn't," he agreed but Murphy continued. "Does your friend, Mr. Katrek make a habit of leaving his $80,000 car with you?
"I'd say it's more like occasionally. Usually when he's going to be out of town for a while. It's cheaper than parking it at the airport, safer too."
"And like you said, there's plenty of room." Laurence Howlund nodded and Murphy took another long look at the actor. Then it hit him, "You're Sal Amato!" He pointed, remembering the bass player from *Eddie and the Cruisers*. Howlund, aka Laurence Matthews aka Matthew Laurence aka Sal Amato, smiled again.

"My dear friend Sal is one of the many men I've been in my life. A character for whom I have a particular affinity. Thank you for recognizing him, detective." Murphy thought about what Judith's reaction would be when he told her he met Sal Amato.

"Is there something else, detective Murphy? That autograph perhaps?" Howlund asked, noticing Murphy was lost in thought.

"I don't think Tom Bergeron was convincing as a piano player," he blurted out. Howlund laughed.

"I'll be sure to tell him you said so next time I see him." With that, the actor pushed himself off the Aston Martin and headed for the front door. "Adios and goodbye, detective," he said with a wave.

Murphy stood there for a minute then walked to his rental car. Inside he wrote down the license plate numbers of the Vanquish and the Grand Cherokee. Next to the Jeep's plate number he wrote the name Brian Katrek. Then he grabbed his phone and made a call to the LAPD's Hollywood Division.

"Good afternoon, this is Detective Murphy and I'm LEO in town working on a case."

"How can the LAPD be of assistance, detective?"

"I was hoping someone could run a plate for me, actually two." He recited the license plate numbers for both vehicles as well as the name of his Commanding Officer and his detective shield number. Then he waited.

"Detective Murphy?"

"Right here."

"The Aston Martin is registered to Lawrence Howlund," Murphy put a check mark next to that number.

"And the Cherokee?" he asked
"That's registered to a Johnny "Jack" Maginnes." Murphy sat stunned.

"Do you have an address for Maginnes?" The officer gave it to him and he noticed it matched the business address Chloe Hill had given him. Murphy thanked the LAPD officer and hung up. He stared at the Jeep Grand Cherokee. "Mr. Maginnes," he said, "why in the world does your name keep popping up with regard to this case?" The answer to his question was a knock on the passenger side door. It startled Murphy, who grabbed for the gun that wasn't currently on his hip. He looked and saw Laurence Howlund/Matthews staring back. Murphy rolled down the window.

"Car trouble, detective? Need a jump?"

"No. No, thanks," Murphy sputtered.

"Why, may I ask, are you still in my driveway?"

"Did you say that SRT belongs to a friend of yours named Brian Katrek?" He didn't answer Howlund's question.

"I did," he replied, "and I also questioned why that was any of your business."

"I'm getting awfully tired of people telling me doing my business is none of my business," he said with more than a hint of anger in his voice. "It's my business because the LAPD says that car," he pointed to the Jeep, "is registered to a private investigator who worked for your sister-in-law, named Johnny Maginnes."

"No kidding," the actor didn't sound surprised or alarmed, "So?"

"So it appears Misters Katrek and Maginnes are the same guy," Murphy concluded.

"Not as far as I'm concerned, detective. I don't know a soul named Johnny Maginnes. The only person I've ever seen drive that car is Brian Katrek."

"How did you and Mr. Katrek become friendly?"

"We met on a movie lot where he was providing security. We talked girls and golf, hit it off." The answer convinced Murphy Murphy that Brian Katrek was indeed Johnny "Jack" Maginnes. He pulled out a business card and handed it to Howlund.

"*If* you hear from your niece and *when* you see Mr. Katrek again, please give me a call."
"Will do," Howlund said as he looked at the card. "Department of Redundancy Department," he said, shaking his head. "Perfect." Murphy rolled up the window and started to back out of the driveway. Laurence Howlund/Laurence Matthews/Matthew Laurence/Sal Amato waved to him for the second time in minutes.

Thousands of miles away DeMaio Turrell and Chuckie Gruber pulled into the radio station parking lot.

"Do you remember the explanation Goosh said we should use if a question about Stray Dog comes up?" Turrell asked before getting out of the car.

It was a fairly common practice for Jeff Giucigiu to set up an interview with the top rock and roll radio stations in town when Serious Crisis came for a concert. The sit downs were, historically, painless and friendly. A half an hour or so with a fawning DJ talking music and records and favorite restaurants in town. Occasionally viewer call-ins were involved. Both Turrell and Gruber had taken part in previous interviews with this station in the past and this disc jockey in particular. She had revealed herself as a fan of the band early on, someone who actually listened to and liked Serious Crisis's music. The band's manager had noticed the DJ's social media posts had recently exhibited a fondness for the group's newest member, Lyndsay Howlund. Because of that he anticipated her asking some questions about her impact on the band and its music. The problem, of course, was that Lyndsay didn't happen to be with the band at the moment. Nobody in the group seemed to have any clue as to why she would leave and where she would go. They just knew for the first time in months they were about to hit the stage without her.

"I remember the gist of it," Gruber answered, "Lyndsay is taking some time to attend to personal family business and therefore won't be performing with us."

'Don't say therefore," Turrell cautioned. "I've known you forever and I've never heard you say therefore."

"Ok," Gruber nodded, "How about consequently, hence, or ergo?" he smiled.

"Yeah ergo. Go with ergo."

"Where do you think she went?" he asked, "Why wouldn't she let anyone know she was leaving?" The second question was one everyone had been asking since that night.

"I don't know." Turrell shook his head. "A few months ago we were having a beer after a show and she told me she wasn't sure the whole rock and roll band thing was where she wanted to be."

"You're kidding?"

"Wish I was. She said she loved the music and all the guys…"

"Even Herbie?" Chuckie said and laughed.

"Even Herbie. But she said all those eyes watching her on stage made her uncomfortable. I told her she'd get used to it."

"We all got used to it," Gruber agreed.

"She wasn't convinced. Said she just might leave, go to L.A. or Nashville, sell her songs and be anonymous."

"She said that?"

"She did, but I made her promise that if, or when, that time came she'd let me know. She said she would."

"Did you tell that detective all of this?" Chuckie sounded worried.

"He never asked."

"Did you believe her?"

"I did."

"And did she tell you the time had come?"

"She did not."

"Man, I hope she's okay," Gruber said.

"We all do Chuckie, we all do. Ready?"

"Ready," Gruber nodded and they both got out of the car.

Murphy Murphy ate a Subway sandwich and then stopped at Seven Grand, a downtown Los Angeles whiskey bar Charlie had recommended. "Ask for Mina," she had said, assuring Murphy if Mina was working he'd be well taken care of. He had just logged on to an online hotel booking site and reserved a room at something called The Ginosi

Wilshire Apartel; $87 a night discounted from $251. The website gave it three and a half stars. He stopped at the bar because the case of Serious Crisis had him bamboozled and he thought an Irish whiskey might help. He picked the hotel because of the price, but he also liked the fact that, according to his phone, it was a fifteen minute walk from Seven Grand in case he decided one Irish wasn't enough.

He had checked in with both Captain Hill and his sister Chloe, and neither had heard from Lyndsay or anyone associated with her disappearance. By "associated", Murphy and the Captain meant a person or persons who may have abducted her and might be looking for compensation as a bargaining chip for her safe return. Murphy understood the concern but had a hard time wrapping his head around the fact that kidnapping was behind this. For the moment it felt to the detective like Lyndsay had just up and left. She'd even thought to grab her Martin guitar, the reason or reasons behind her departure remaining a mystery. Neither he nor either of the Hills seemed at all eager to consider anything more sinister than a kidnapping for ransom plot on one end of the spectrum and a runaway rock star on the other.

The detective had also told the Captain about the strange circumstance of the possible dual identity of Katrek and Maginnes, as well as how the actor

Laurence Mathews did, or didn't, fit in. He wanted the captain to feel like he was making progress. He made sure to sound convincing. Apparently it worked because Hill made no mention of Vance Veezy and his missing persons team. They agreed that both the Captain and the mother would attempt to contact the private investigator and Hill left it to Murphy to deal with the movie star. Captain Hill suggested a plan to have Chloe reach out to Maginnes and dangle the promise of unpaid services as a carrot to entice him out in the open. Murphy agreed at the time that it was an idea worth pursuing.

Inside the less than crowded bar he pulled up a chair. A check of his watch told Murphy it was not yet five pm but that was local time and his body clock was running a couple of hours later. More than late enough for a drink.

"What can I get you?" A striking Asian woman, dressed head to toe in black, addressed the detective.

"Are you Mina?" Murphy asked, noticing the bartender sported no name tag and wondering if she was the person Charlie Carlucci had mentioned.

"I am not," she answered, "Mina's off tonight. I'm Shizuko." Murphy thought that was a pretty name and he told her as much. "Thank you. It means 'quiet child'".

"I'm Murphy," he told her, "and as far as I know it doesn't mean a darn thing." That made Shizuko laugh.

"What's your pleasure Mr. Murphy?"

"I'll have an Irish whiskey, Jameson, neat please," he answered
"How perfectly pedestrian." She seemed to insult Murphy in the nicest possible way.

"Do you have a better suggestion?" Murphy asked taking no offense.

"About a hundred of them," she said, waving her hand like Vanna White on Wheel of Fortune across the bottles behind the bar.

"You choose," he deferred

"Omakase? I like it."

"I'm sorry Oma what?" Murphy asked

"Omakase," She answered, "In Japanese it means respectfully leaving a decision up to another to decide what's best but I guess it's more commonly known as chef's choice."

"Omakase it is," Murphy lightly slapped the bar and smiled.

She turned toward the bottle revealing the fact that the black shirt she was wearing had no back. Murphy suddenly missed Charlie more than ever. When Shizuko turned back around, she was holding a bottle. The label identified it as a Midleton Irish Whiskey. Murphy recognized the brand as the same one he had enjoyed with his friend Mal Turner but this bottle was different. Under the distiller's name the label read Barry Crockett Legacy. She pulled the cork and poured a healthy bit of it into a heavy crystal glass.

"Enjoy," she said and walked away. Murphy sipped and thought. His first thought was that the whiskey was delicious, even better than Turner's. His next thought turned to Lyndsay Howlund. Until this case he had no personal experience with kidnappings or runaways but he knew, from research, expert opinions, and officers with firsthand knowledge, that every day that passed made it exponentially more difficult for law enforcement to reach a favorable resolution. While he couldn't be certain something terrible hadn't already happened to the young woman, he willed himself to believe otherwise. Regardless, he couldn't shake the gut feeling that Johnny "Jack" Maginnes, aka Brian Katrek, was involved. He needed to find him and he needed to find him fast. He had listened to the Captain's idea about drawing Maginnes out using Chloe Hill. He didn't argue or object but he also didn't think it would work. Maginnes was a cool customer and Murphy guessed he knew exactly how much the Captain's sister had paid him and whether she still owed him more. The detective didn't say so but he surmised the best way to find the private eye was through the actor, Laurence Matthews. He just had to figure out how to do it.

"How's the Crockett?" Shizuko was back. Murphy told her it was delicious, because it was, and he ordered a refill. The bartender poured round two in a different, equally clean and heavy crystal glass.

Another sip, a different thought. The guitar tech, Marty Kaufmann, said he and Lyndsay had a disagreement on stage about how her acoustic guitar sounded. He intimated it wasn't exactly a fight, just a difference of opinion. Had someone else been privy to it? Murphy realized he failed to ask Kaufmann that question. He grabbed his phone and called Jeff Giucigiu.

"Hello, this is Jeff," the manager sounded busy.

"Jeff, this is Detective Murphy."

"Oh, hello detective. Are you calling with good news?" Murphy thought on how quickly he went from busy to hopeful.

"I'm afraid not," Murphy had to admit.

"That sucks. So, what can I do for you?"

"Is Marty Kaufmann back with the band?"
"He is. Came back yesterday and believe me we're all pleasantly pleased about that."

"May I speak with him?" Murphy asked skipping the rebuke.

"He's a little busy right at the moment. Show's about to start."

"The band has a concert tonight?" Murphy wondered if he had forgotten or if he never knew.

"First one without Lyndsay. It should be pretty weird."

"No doubt," Murphy agreed, "Will you have Mr. Kaufmann call me at his earliest convenience." It was a statement, not a question.

"Of course, but it might be late."

"Doesn't matter. Thanks Jeff and have a good show."

"Appreciate that detective." They hung up. Murphy guessed the world, at least the world around rock and roll, was about to learn that Lyndsay Howlund wasn't where she was supposed to be. He also speculated that his job was about to get that much more difficult.

Murphy asked for and received the check and recoiled a little when he saw the tab. *No wonder it tastes so good* he thought as he plopped down his credit card. He thanked Shizuko, who said she hoped she'd see him again. He doubted she would, but just nodded in response before he walked the handful of blocks to his hotel. From the outside he realized why they called it an "Apartel". He scolded himself for not putting two and two together earlier. The building was an apartment building that some enterprising person or corporation decided would be more lucrative if they could rent the rooms by the night instead of the month. Murphy didn't really care as long as it had hot and cold running water, a functioning toilet and clean sheets on a bed. To his satisfaction the building had all three and the price was certainly right. Once upstairs he changed into sleeping attire, wrote some notes in his book, and turned on the television. He flipped around before settling on a college basketball game; he had no idea if it was live or prerecorded from a different era and he didn't care. His mind raced as he thought about how best to approach Laurence Matthews and finally decided the direct approach would be the best approach. That settled he dozed until his ringing phone interrupted that.

"Murphy," he surprised himself at how alert he sounded.
"Detective, this is Marty Kaufmann."

"Mr. Kaufmann. Thanks for calling. How are you feeling?"

"Fine," he answered. Murphy thought he sounded tired. "But I'm going to take a shot in the dark and say you didn't want me to call to tell you what condition my condition is in." Murphy gave him a pass on the redundancy because he knew and liked the old Kenny Rogers and the First Edition song.

"Actually I do care," Murphy countered, "but you're right."

"No disrespect detective but I'd appreciate you getting right to it then. I'm beat."

"No problem," Murphy got right to it, "Did anyone else see you quarreling with Miss Howlund the night she went missing?"

"I wouldn't call it a quarrel," he pushed back, "Like I told you, more like a mild disagreement."

"Fair enough."

"And... let me think," he paused, "Smitty was right there, so I guess him." He paused again. Murphy could hear the air whistling as Kaufmann breathed through his nose. "Oh, and Mags."

"Johnny Maginnes?"

"Is that his name?"

"It is. And he was there?"

"Sure, he was around a lot."

"Backstage after the show?"

"I didn't see him backstage," Kaufmann corrected, "but he was right there next to the stage, by Lyndsay, throughout the entire show. No doubt in my mind he heard us talking."

"Didn't you find it odd that he could get so close? Where was security?"

"Mags had long since buddied up to our security guys and my guess is they approved of him favorably and then told the local guys that he was good. He was right there during most shows. In fact, if I were a gambling man I'd wager a bet that he had a thing for her."

"For Lyndsay? He looks like he's old enough to be her father."

"Don't judge detective. Don't judge. Anyway, I'm not a gambler so I don't have to risk any of my fortune."

"Interesting," Murphy thought about what Kaufmann had said. "Thanks for your time Marty, I really appreciate it. Call back if you think of anything else. And Marty?"

"Yes, detective?"

"Please take care of yourself."

"Thanks. I plan on it."

After the call Murphy Murphy tossed and turned and chewed on what Kaufmann had said. He propped up his lumpy pillow and half sat up in bed. He thought for a bit about what he would say to Laurence Matthews the next day. He reached for his phone and called his friend Judith Colman.

"Hullo," Murphy knew immediately he had awakened her and regretted being so selfish.

"Oh geez, Jude. I'm really sorry."

"Murph?"

"Go back to sleep," he insisted, "I'll call you tomorrow."

"Don't be silly," she said, "I'm awake now. Where are you?"

"Los Angeles," He answered, "Didn't you get my message?"

"Yeah. No. I don't know. What are you doing in L.A.?"

"Trying to find Lyndsay Howlund."

"Oh, right. How can I help?" she asked, now wide awake. Murphy brought her up to speed on the case; what he found, what he didn't find, to whom he hadn't spoken and who he had, including Lyndsay's uncle.

"Did you know he's Sal Amato?"

"Sal, the bass player from *Eddie and the Cruisers*?"

"The same."

"Holy cannoli, Murphy. You gotta get his autograph… For the bar of course."

"Of course," Murphy chuckled. "I'm going back to see him tomorrow…"

"I'll text you to remind you about the autograph," she interrupted, "Get him to sign a picture. To me, uh I mean to The Pizzer."

"Okay Jude, please calm down," he attempted to bring her back to earth, "I called because I need your help."

"Oh. Right. Sorry."

"Thanks. Mr. Howlund knows his niece is missing, but, quite frankly, he didn't appear to be all that concerned about it. Does that set off any alarms for you?

"Not really," Judith said after thinking for a moment.

"Really? Why?"

First off the guy's an actor, and a dang good one if you ask me, and you just hit him with a two by four.

I'm not sure how you expected him to act, in that moment, in front of a total stranger and I have no idea how he reacted, in the privacy of his home, after you left."

"Good point," Murphy conceded. "What about this whole Maginnes, Katrek, car in the driveway, business?"

"Now *that's* a mystery," Judith agreed, "Why would that guy use an alias with a good friend?"

"Why do you say he's a good friend?"

"Didn't you tell me this Maginnes guy parked his $80,000 car in Sal's driveway?"

"I did."

"That's no acquaintance, I can tell you that. I think a deeper dig is in order on that front."

"Excellent idea," Murphy concurred, "now go back to sleep, Judith. And thanks."

"No worries, Murphy, happy to help but I'm wide awake now. Namath! Bear! You guys want to go for a walk?" Murphy heard her call to the dogs and he hung up. He fell asleep more convinced than ever

that Johnny "Jack" Maginnes was at the heart of this
whole mystery.

Murphy Murphy Greets Another Day Hoping to Get Answers To His Questions

The detective's sleep was interrupted by an occasional passing siren and a less than optimal pillow. Nonetheless, Murphy Murphy rose the next morning feeling surprisingly refreshed. He showered, shaved and dressed, then walked toward Seven Grand and his rental car. Along the way he called to check in with Charlie. He told her downtown L.A. had changed since he'd been there last but most everything else appeared the same. Then he told her he missed her.

"Did you run into Mina?" she had asked

"Unfortunately no, but the bar was worthy of your recommendation."

"When are you coming home?"

"Depends," he'd answered. "A day or two if I get lucky. Sooner than that if I don't."

"Well then I'll grudgingly wish you luck. I'd love to have you back here but I'd prefer you solve this case." Murphy thanked her and said he'd check back when he could. He reached his rental, happy to find it undisturbed, and drove off.

Through the years he'd found it easier for him to think in two places; a record store or a library. He knew the big Tower Records store on Sunset had long since closed so he headed toward 5th street and the Los Angeles Public Library. It was built in the 1920's and Murphy remembered reading, at one time, that it was the third largest public library in the country behind The Library of Congress and The New York Public Library. He wondered if it still was. He did know for a fact that it featured outdoor gardens, fountains, and reflecting pools that helped get one's thoughts in order. Murphy checked his watch and felt it was too early to call a movie star, even a B-list one, so he parked his car, purchased a newspaper, and entered the building.

Before opening the paper, he opened the search engine on his phone to see if Serious Crisis had made any news. Sure enough a quick google yielded two internet stories about the band's concert the previous night. Both were solid, if not spectacular, and each mentioned that Lyndsay Howlund had not been part of the show. Murphy read to the end and found neither writer made much of the absence apparently buying some pre-determined story about personal business that needed attention. Murphy knew that gave him a little more time but he worried about how much. He got up and moved to an equally pretty, slightly less sunny spot and started reading the newspaper. Forty minutes later he decided it would be acceptable to call Laurence Matthews.

"Go ahead caller," Murphy heard the actor's voice and thought it sounded like the man had been awake for hours.

"Mr. Matthews or Howlund, this is Detective Murphy."

"I know. I recognized the number from your business card. Do you think I always answer my phone, 'go ahead caller'?"

"I'm sure I have no idea."

"What can I do for you on the fine Southern California day?" The man sounded positively chipper and that made Murphy angry.

"You can help me find your niece," was all he had to say.

They agreed to meet an hour later at a place called the Beachwood Café. Murphy knew it, since he'd eaten there before. He remembered it was practically right underneath the famous Hollywood sign, or at least you could see it from the sidewalk. Murphy figured it was about a fifteen minute drive so he finished reading the paper.

He arrived at the restaurant before Howlund, so he approached the young lady who served as the hostess and told her there would be two of them. She checked a clipboard and informed Murphy they were "filled to capacity" and because he didn't have "advanced reservations" it would be fifteen or twenty minutes, "maybe a half an hour" but she would do everything she could to get them seated "as soon as possible". The detective had several reasons not to like the girl but one, in particular, was that he noticed several empty tables, despite the fact that a handful of folks, who he determined were tourists, waited with him outside. A woman wearing an Abilene Christian University sweatshirt smiled at him and he smiled back.

A few minutes later Laurence Howlund arrived. Murphy was a little surprised to see he wasn't driving the Aston Martin. Instead the actor was behind the wheel of an impeccable, beautifully restored, blue 1957 Chevy Bel Air. It appeared to Murphy to be the same car Eddie Wilson drove in *Eddie and the Cruisers*. He saw an only slightly older looking Sal Amato from the movie smile as he drove past and parked. As he got out of the car and walked toward the restaurant the detective noticed he wore jeans, a plain white t-shirt covered by a sports coat, and a pair of bright red Adidas Gazelle shoes. The two men shook hands.

"Is that?" Murphy pointed at the Chevy.

"Maybe," the actor said, "maybe not. Let's eat."

"The hostess said it could be a half an hour wait. That was ten minutes ago."

"Did she?" he turned and walked toward the entrance. Murphy fell in behind him.

"Oh hey Mr. Matthews," the girl greeted Howlund.

"Hello Courtney. How are the acting lessons going?"

"Great! I feel like I'm learning a ton and the teacher said her approach is extremely unique." The phrase set off alarm bells inside Murphy's head. It was, by far, his least favorite redundancy. "Today I'm going to be an elephant!" she suddenly hunched over and swung her right arm back and forth across her body.

"Good old Strasberg," Howlund said smiling, "I'm sure you'll do great."

"May I offer a word of advice?" Murphy leaned in between the two.

"Are you an actor too?" The girl excitedly asked

"I consider myself more a teacher," Murphy answered, "and I would run as far away from your current one as your little legs will take you."

"What? Why?" the girl looked mortified.

"Because there are no degrees of uniqueness young lady. Something is either unique or it isn't." Murphy leaned back out. The girl looked at the detective and then at the actor. Howlund shrugged his shoulders.

"Your table is right this way," she said as she led them into the restaurant.

A waitress set down two glasses of water and a couple of menus.

"Minestrone soup is the soup du jour today," she informed them and then asked if either wanted coffee. Howlund did, Murphy, who was afraid he might lose his appetite, asked for tea.

"This place isn't as good as it used to be," the actor said apologetically.

"You can say that about a lot of things," Murphy added, "Have you been to a P.F. Chang's lately?"

"Can't say that I have," the actor answered. "Anyhow, the eggs benedict are still very good and the mixed berry pancakes are excellent."

"Good to know," the detective said. A different waitress came by to take their order.

"Hi Mr. Matthews," she said, pulling a pencil from her apron, "Mixed berry cakes and a large, cold, glass of milk?" she asked, already writing.

"Sounds like a plan."

"And for your teacher friend?" she turned to Murphy, who thought word travelled fast at the Beachwood Café.

"Make it two," he offered, "but no milk for me." She smiled and walked away. "I take it you're a regular," he said to Howlund.

"It's good to have a place," was the response, "don't you think, detective? Now you said you thought I could help you find my niece."

"I said I wanted you to help me find your niece," Murphy corrected him.

"Semantics," the actor waved his hand in front of his face. "How, pray tell, do you think I know where she is?"

"I don't know that you do," Murphy looked the actor in the eyes, "but I'm pretty darn sure your friend Mr. Katrek does."

"Is that a fact or a hunch?"

"Not a fact, no sir, nor a hunch. Call it an educated guess and I've been thinking long and hard about it and in my mind it all adds up." He went through the timeline of when he believed Katrek, or as Murphy Murphy knew him, Maginnes, started showing up at Serious Crisis shows. Howlund, for his part, supplemented the story with when and how he met the man. It turned out dropping off the Jeep coincided with several Serious Crisis show dates.

Their food came and they dug in. Murphy conceded the pancakes were, indeed, "excellent". The detective also told Lyndsay's uncle what Marty Kaufmann had said about Maginnes possibly having a crush on his niece.

"I'd put your Maginnes and my Katrek at mid to late forties, maybe even fifty," Howlund had said, "That's old enough to be Lyndsay's father."

"Tell me about him," Murphy asked, "Lyndsay's father."

"Tony," Howlund said and then he finished his glass of milk. "It's better if you drink it when it's still really cold," he said, then he licked his upper lip.

"Tony Howlund," Murphy prompted.

"My baby brother," the actor said, no longer thinking about cold milk. "I was nine, maybe almost ten, when he was born." Murphy could see the actor remembering. "Unexpected surprise," he smiled a small smile.

"Are there other kinds?"

"Other kinds of what?"

"Surprises. Aren't they all, by definition, *unexpected*?"

"Now that you mention it, I guess they are," the actor nodded. "Anyhow, baby Tony was a surprise, and not in a good way at least as far as I was concerned. Never liked him much."

"Did he know that?"

"Hard for him not to know. I was a terrible brother. You see detective, I knew fairly early on what I wanted to do with my life. I saw a couple of movies; one featuring Paul Newman and another starring Steve McQueen. I was hooked. I wanted to be them, or whatever version of them I could be, and nothing was going to stand in my way. Especially a kid brother."

"So, what happened to him?"

"I mostly didn't know and at the time I really didn't care. I told you I was a bad brother. I left home the minute I thought I could without someone coming to look for me. I never looked, or went, back." Murphy took a sip of his now cold tea as the actor kept going. "I waited tables, got some small parts in community theatres, put myself through acting school. Once a year, at or close to her birthday, I'd call my mom." He looked at Murphy and shrugged again. "You can't blame a guy for missing his mom, can you?"

"No, you can't," Murphy said, thinking about his mother.
"When we ran out of pleasantries, which was pretty quickly, she told me about Tony. 'Tony can ride a two-wheeler, Tony's got a girlfriend, Tony's playing football. Tony set the state record. Tony's joining the Army. Tony's getting married.' I still didn't care. Then a few birthdays later she answered the phone

and started crying. She told me she was going to be a grandma. Tony was having a baby, I was an uncle. Suddenly I cared, about the kid that is. I cared about my niece."

Murphy thought it was quite the story. He thought about Judith saying Laurence Matthews was a 'darn good' actor and wondered about how much of the story was true. Fact or fiction Murphy conceded that he admired the way he told it.

"Then one day Tony was gone. Volunteered for active duty and that was the last any of us, me, Mom, Chloe, Lyndsay, heard from Tony Howlund." He sat back. Murphy thought he looked drained.

"Did you know Mr. Maginnes was ex-military?" Laurence Howlund stared off into space and Murphy wondered if he'd heard the question.

"He told me. Said it was how he got the job on the movie set so easily. But even if he hadn't told me it was pretty obvious."
"How well did you know this guy?"
"I don't know, pretty well. He took great care of us on the set, very professional. And as it turned out, we had a number of things in common."

"You weren't suspicious of that?"

"Not ever. Didn't cross my mind."

"Did you ever go to his home? Did you go out to lunch or dinner? Did you watch football games? Play golf?"

"Some of that, over time, sure," Howlund nodded, "but I've never been to his home. I do remember going to a place over on Pico with him a number of times. Seemed like it was his spot, his place."

"Recently?"

"A month maybe six weeks ago was the last time. He and one of the bartenders seemed pretty friendly."

"Could you find it again?"

"Easy."

The two agreed to meet again that evening. Murphy would come to Howlund's home and they would head over to the bar on Pico together. That gave Murphy another afternoon in L.A.. He filled part of it by finding a record store, actually two. He stopped first at Rockaway Records and then at Vacation Vinyl. That was where he came across Mozart's Piano Concerto No. 20 and 24 performed by Claire Haskil and the Orchestre des Concerts Lamoureux. It was a recording he didn't have, but one he wanted, so he figured why not buy it.

As he was admiring the copy a man wearing a hoodie that covered much of his face entered the store and moved with a purpose toward the cash register on the counter. Murphy Murphy decided his purpose was a robbery. The detective put down the record and grabbed one of the many bongs that were on display throughout the store. This one had elaborate piping and a heavy glass bottom. He quietly moved toward the would-be thief.

"Give me all your cash money!" the hoodie called. The kid behind the counter froze. "Your alternative choice is to get shot," he added, pulling a pistol from his pocket.

"Hang on! Hang on, Dude!" the kid was scared to death, "Just let me get the register open."

"Hurry up! Don't make me circle around there and do it myself!"

That was it for Murphy. It was bad enough the guy was trying to rob a record store but the constant use of redundancies pushed the detective over the edge. He moved in behind the thief and smacked him on the head with the bong. The hoodie went down like a ton of bricks.

"Call the police," he said to the kid.

"Dude! You just knocked that armed gunman out cold! What are you some kind of former veteran or something?"

"Something," Murphy said thinking about beating the kid with the bong. "Call 9-1-1," Murphy added as he reached into his pocket and pulled out a fifty dollar bill. "This is for the Mozart record and this bong," he put the bill on the counter. "Now call the police." Murphy left the store and went to a movie.

He located a theatre in Santa Monica that was showing a matinee of *Cool Hand Luke* starring Paul Newman. He didn't know if this was one of the performances to which Laurence Howlund referred but he decided it certainly could be. He bought a ticket and a bucket of popcorn at the counter and went in.

The film was made in 1967, making Newman twenty two years old at the time. Murphy had seen the legendary actor's work in *Butch Cassidy and the Sundance Kid*, *The Sting*, and *Slap Shot*, all long after he had decided law enforcement was his calling. As he watched the young actor become Lucas "Luke" Jackson, a role for which he earned both an Academy Award and a Golden Globe Award nomination for best actor, he wondered if he had instead seen it as an impressionable pre-teen would he have done what Howlund did. He thought probably not, but he understood why the actor did.

After the movie he enjoyed a chopped salad at a place called Tender Greens and decided it was time to brave the traffic on the way back to the Hollywood Hills. He guessed it would take as long as ninety minutes to get there and it did. While waiting in bumper to bumper traffic, Murphy went over his strategy if and when he and Matthews encountered Maginnes. If they didn't run across the private eye Murphy had made up his mind that a more experienced officer should be brought in to take over the case. It wasn't because he thought he couldn't find Lyndsay Howlund, he just doubted his ability, thanks to his lack of experience in this area, to find her in time. Vance Veezy and his missing persons team were simply better equipped. Murphy Murphy knew a young woman and her family deserved better equipped. He shook his head remembering this all started with a stolen, two thousand dollar, cigarette lighter.

If they did meet up with Maginnes, and Murphy said a silent prayer that they would, the detective determined the plan would be he would confront the man first, hit him with every question and piece of evidence, circumstantial or not, and then have Howlund come in for round two. It would then be the actor's role to establish the fact that Maginnes, or

Katrek as he knew him, was deceptive at best, an outright liar at least, and a kidnapper at worst. If necessary, Murphy would take one last turn at him. He knew it was a long shot but he thought it was the last shot he had. He hoped the actor would agree to the plan and give an award winning performance. Murphy wasn't sure Howlund would say yes, partly because he still wasn't one hundred percent sure the actor wasn't involved somehow. He'd find out soon enough.

When he took the exit off the 101 he called Laurence Howlund and told him he was close. Once again the gate at 7974 Woodrow Wilson Drive was open and Murphy pulled in. He noticed immediately the Grand Cherokee was gone and the Vanquish was nowhere in sight. In its place was a plain black BMW 530i. The space in the driveway previously occupied by the white SRT was empty, so Murphy put his rental in its place. Laurence Howlund came out of the house at the same time Murphy exited his car.

"Jeep's gone," Murphy stated the obvious.

"Wasn't here when I returned from our rendezvous together," Howlund said, getting into the beemer. Murphy got in too.

"Don't you think that's something I should know?"

"You know now," the actor buckled his seat belt and started the car. "Would knowing a handful of hours earlier have made any difference?" Murphy couldn't think of a reason it would have. He buckled up as well.

"Nice car," he said.

"This? I guess," Howlund smiled. "It's my running around town when you want to look like everyone else running around town, car."

"So, this is a common vehicle around here?" That made the actor laugh out loud.

"Haven't you noticed? They're everywhere. This or a Mercedes G-Class." Murphy hadn't noticed but he decided to keep his eyes peeled. "You know the overused cliché," Howlund continued, "If you don't want to stand out in the crowd, be a part of the crowd."

"That's not a cliché, and don't do that," Murphy said calmly.

"Do what?" Howlund asked, even though he knew what.

"Use a redundant phrase just to get a rise out of me."

"Apologies detective. Won't happen again. I'll completely eradicate them from my vocabulary."

"Let's go," Murphy stared straight ahead.

On the way, Murphy laid out his plan. Howlund not only agreed, he thought it was an excellent course of action, but told Murphy he appreciated the extra time he would have to "get into character". Murphy admitted that if they didn't find Maginnes, or couldn't get him to admit to anything, the next step would be to tell his Captain to call in the reinforcements. Howlund thought that was the right approach too. They left the Hollywood Hills and the BMW turned left onto Sunset. He told Murphy if they stayed on the famous street it would take them all the way through Beverly Hills. Murphy said he didn't care. Howlund turned left onto LaCienega and hit more stop and go traffic.

"Was it *Cool Hand Luke*?" Murphy asked.
"Was what *Cool Hand Luke*?"

"The movie that made you want to be an actor?"

"Oh that. Sure, it was Luke and it was *Hud*, but mostly it was *The Hustler*. And those were just the Newman films. Have you seen Brando in *Viva Zapata* or *The Wild One* or *The Godfather*?"

"I liked Butch Cassidy," Murphy offered.

"Who didn't?" They drove on through a few more traffic lights. "Do you really think my friend Brian Katrek did something to Lyndsay?"

"I hope not with all my heart," Murphy said honestly, "but if he didn't I have absolutely no idea who might have."

Despite the traffic they made decent time. They turned left onto Pico and Howlund pointed to a sign up ahead on the right. It was bright red neon and it read, The Barrel.

"That's it," the actor said proudly, "I'll park."

Murphy thought the building was less than impressive, but the fading light of another Southern California day was. Pinks and yellows and shades of purple and blue silhouetted a handful of palm trees lining the street. A couple of them looked to Murphy like dandelion flowers gone to seed waiting for a giant to come by and blow them on their way. He refreshed his memory as to what Maginnes looked like, long hair and short, and rehearsed in his head the first few lines. Laurence Howlund gave him all the space he needed and he knew the drill. For the first time he could remember Murphy wished he had his gun.

"If you don't see me back here within fifteen minutes, I'll see you in there." Murphy got out of the BMW.

"Good Luck, Murphy," Howlund offered as the detective closed the door.

The Case of Serious Crisis Takes a Turn With No Advanced Warning

Murphy stood at the door and sucked in a deep breath. Adrenaline had already started running through his veins. He knew he needed to calm down a bit before a face to face with Maginnes. He also was aware that there was a better than decent chance the man wouldn't even be inside. One more breath and he pulled open the door.

It was dark inside but after just a few seconds the detective's eyes adjusted. The room had low ceilings and an old wood floor. At first glance it looked to Murphy like there were three rows of small circular tables, maybe big enough for five or six people if they didn't mind sitting shoulder to shoulder. The tables fronted a stage that was raised a handful of inches off the ground. There was a scaled down drum kit (a kick drum, a snare and a cymbal) in one corner of the stage and a stool with a microphone stand in front of it at its center. Murphy calculated that you could maybe get one hundred and fifty humans in the space but only if quite a few of them were skinny. It felt half the size of Charlie's bar.

There were several framed pictures on the wall, with some filled with photographs of artists Murphy recognized; Jackson Browne, Stevie Wonder, Tom Jones. As Murphy took another look around the room he tried to imagine any of them performing on that stage, in this building. There was also an A rating from the city health department displayed proudly behind the bar. A redhead stood next to it staring at Murphy. He made a move toward her, sat on a stool and said hello. On the bar, two seats to his left, was a half-drunk, large snifter of dark beer. One look at the taps told Murphy it was probably a Guinness. He hoped that was a good sign. A couple occupied two more stools at the bar farther down. Murphy took another look around the room. Several of the tables were occupied, a fact that hadn't registered with Murphy when he first entered. Maybe it was the darkness, maybe he was distracted, maybe the people came in after him. He turned back to the bar and the redhead was directly in front of him.

"Welcome to The Bucket, officer. What can I get you?"

It didn't bother Murphy that she pegged him for a cop. He was there on cop business and he wasn't trying to pretend to be anything else. In fact, he wore it like a badge of honor as he showed the redhead his shield.

"I'm Detective Murphy and I'll have a Jameson, neat."

"Very good," she smiled, "By the way, I'm Dina." She grabbed a glass and the bottle of whiskey and poured Murphy his drink.

"Live music tonight?" he asked.

"Is today a day that ends in y?" she answered. "That'll be ten bucks. You want to settle up or open a tab?"

"Why not," Murphy reached in his pocket for a credit card, "No idea how long I'll be here." He slid the card her way.

"We close at three," she said while pickup up the card.

"I'm looking for somebody who may spend a fair bit of time in here," he told her back. She turned around.

"Is that so?" she asked. Murphy nodded. "This somebody have a name?" She put her hands in her pockets and leaned back against the shelves that held bottles of tequila, vodka and gin.

"More than one, I'm afraid."
"Is that so?" she asked again.

"Some people know him as Brian Katrek. To others he's Johnny, John or Jack Maginnes and there may be more. Any of those names ring a bell?" The redhead smiled.

"Hello again Detective," Maginnes said as he plopped down in front of his beer. "Thanks Dina," he said, lifting his glass her way in a toast. Murphy picked up his glass and moved next to the private investigator.

"I've been looking for you," he said.

"Not surprised," was all Maginnes offered. Murphy pulled out his phone and typed a text to Howlund asking the actor to wait outside for a few more minutes and hit send.

"Look, Mr. Maginnes, I think, in the past, you and I have had a failure to communicate," Murphy remembered the line from *Cool Hand Luke*. "I'd like to remedy that. Where's Lyndsay Howland?" Maginnes answered by taking a long pull from his beer. Murphy leaned a little closer. "As far as I can tell you were one of the last people, if not *the* last person, to see her. I've spoken to everyone else that was there that night and I have a pretty good sense that they are telling me the truth. Now I'm talking to you, Johnny. Where's the girl?"

Maginnes closed his eyes. Murphy pushed harder.

"Were the two of you romantically involved? Did you want to be but she rejected your advances?

"What?" Maginnes seemed genuinely surprised. "Are you out of your mind? I'm old enough to be that girl's father." Murphy recalled Marty Kaufmann and Laurence Howlund echoing that sentiment.

"So why did you take her?" Murphy decided to throw a haymaker. With the question, Maginnes turned to stare at Murphy. The detective could see him ball his left hand into a fist. The investigator's face reddened with anger.

"I don't appreciate this line of questioning Mr. Murphy," Maginnes practically spat the words. "You're on very thin ice here and if you keep it up you may not like the end result." Murphy bit his lip and waited a few seconds, hoping Maginnes would cool down.

"Do you know where she is John?"

"Yes."
With that one word Murphy Murphy's mind filled with equal parts relief and dread. He hated to ask his next question but he knew he had to.

"Is she okay John?" Murphy held his breath.

"Yes. What do you think I've got her tied and gagged down at the boat marina or I dropped her down an empty hole somewhere? Geez detective." The dread Murphy felt began to dissipate while his annoyance at Maginnes escalated. "But I didn't take her anywhere Mr. Murphy," he continued "I never forced her to do anything."

"Don't lie to me Johnny. Tell me where she is or take me to her right now." Just then Dina approached.

"You fellas okay? Need another?"

"Sure D," Maginnes said, draining what was left of his beer. He slid the glass her way and smiled. Murphy was agitated by the interruption but the interaction made him think about Howlund saying he thought his friend "had a thing" for a bartender.

"I'm good," Murphy said and waited for an answer from Maginnes that didn't come. Dina poured then served his beer. He thanked her, took a drink and turned to Murphy.
"I told you I'm old enough to be Lyndsay Howlund's father."

"I remember," Murphy acknowledged, "but in this day and age I'm not sure why that makes a difference."

"It makes a difference because Tony Howlund was my brother." The anger rose in Murphy and he shook his head.

"You're such a liar Maginnes and I think we're done here. I'm calling LAPD and we're going to continue this conversation in a different setting." Murphy grabbed his phone again and started punching in numbers. Maginnes reached over with his right hand and stopped him.

"I'm not lying."

"I know for a fact you are John Maginnes. Or is it Brian Katrek?" The fact that Murphy knew Maginnes's alias seemed to confuse the man.

"How? Where did you hear that name?" he sputtered.

"From Tony Howlund's *real* brother Laurence. He's right outside, probably be in here any minute."
"I'm not lying," he said again, this time even more sincerely. "You are correct, we weren't blood but we were brothers. Army. Special Forces."

"You served together?"

"For years. Africa mostly. Gabon, Kenya, the Congo, Tanzania. Wherever Uncle Sam needed us, we went."

"How did he die?" Murphy wondered.

"Didn't know he was dead." That answer caught Murphy by surprise.

"His family claims he joined up but never came back."

"Doesn't mean he's dead."

"But…" Murphy started.

"We had been in country for a while when all of the sudden orders came down that we were going home. Night before we were set to ship out Tony came to me and said he had decided to stay."

"Is that even possible?"

"If you're good and smart, anything is possible Detective. And Tony Howlund was both."

"So, you came home and he didn't."

"Eventually. The fact that he went AWOL upset the apple cart for a while but finally the Pentagon said it was time to go."

"And you never heard from him again?"

"Not a word, but before he left he made one request of me."

"Which was?"

"He asked me to look after his little girl."

"And you agreed." It wasn't a question.

"Without hesitation. The man saved my life more than once. Like I said, he was my brother."

"I'm not saying I believe you but let's say all that's true, I'm still waiting for an answer to *my* request, Mr. Maginnes. Take me to her."

"I can't do that."

"Hello Brian. Or should I call you Johnny?" Laurence Howlund had joined the conversation.

"Hey Laurence. Thanks for taking care of my Jeep," Maginnes greeted him.

"Why don't you join us for a drink, Mr. Howlund?" it was Murphy, "We're making great progress." Dina was back and Howlund ordered.

"Hello there, Red. I'd greatly appreciate a Woodford Reserve Double Batch, neat." Dina looked at him like he was speaking Swahili. "It's bourbon."

"Got it," Dina said, "We don't got it. Will a double Basil Hayden be okay?"

"Doesn't matter if it's okay, Red. I'm an actor, I can act like it's okay."

"I'll take that as a yes," she said to Howlund. "You three going to have dinner and stay for the show?" she asked the group. The question made Murphy turn. The tables in the room were now full, people talking, laughing, enjoying each other's company. It had all happened when he and Maginnes were talking. Howlund sat on the barstool putting Maginnes between him and Murphy Murphy.

"So Johnny, why the heck did you tell me your name was Brian Katrek?"

Maginnes explained that he came to work security on Howlund's movie set because a rival studio had hired him to dig up some dirt on the company that was making that film. He thought it would be better to use a different name in case someone got suspicious and wanted to learn more about him.

"After a few years didn't you think we were good enough friends for you to tell me your real name? Howlund had asked.

"By that time I couldn't figure out why it would matter," Katrek/Maginnes responded. They continued back and forth for several minutes.

"This is all fascinating but can we please get back to Lyndsay? Where is she Johnny?"

Just then Murphy heard a drumstick beat on a snare and then tap on a cymbal. Murphy slapped the bar in frustration at being interrupted again. The drummer's noise made him turn and look at the stage where he saw a young man with longish hair and a scraggly beard holding the drumsticks. He also saw a girl who looked to be about Lyndsay Howlund's age. It could be her he thought, trying to recall the Lyndsay he had met, but her hair was cut short and dyed a deep magenta. She wore a black leather jacket over a black t-shirt and had on bright pink tights. Black calf-high Doc Martens boots were on her feet. A Martin acoustic guitar balanced on her lap as she adjusted the microphone stand.

"Right there," Maginnes said.

Murphy looked at Laurence Howlund, who stared at the girl and then turned his gaze back to the detective. He shrugged his shoulders in a "I don't know, could be her" kind of gesture. Then the girl spoke into the microphone.

"Hi everybody. Thanks for coming out tonight. I know you're not here to see us…" the crowd murmured its agreement. "Pandora's Box will be out shortly…" this time cheers, whistles and hoots interrupted her speech. Lyndsay laughed. "Anyway, I'm," she stopped and thought for a moment, not like she had forgotten her name, more like she was searching for a different one. "Um I'm Tedi and the guy over there," she pointed at the drummer, "well, he's Teddy too. We're Stray Dogs and we're gonna play a few songs that I wrote. This first one is called *Disappear from Sight*. Hope you like it."

The three men sat mesmerized as Lyndsay gave the Martin one last tune before Teddy counted her in.

You sent a bouquet of flowers
I sat and stared at it for hours.
I felt surrounded on all sides
My heart breaking like waves with the tides.
I wanted to fly through the air and avoid this fight
Just hide behind the curtain and disappear from sight."

Elation flooded over Murphy. He was certain he had never been so happy to hear a voice utter a redundant phrase. He got up and made his way outside to call Chloe Hill.

"Hello," she answered on the first ring. Murphy heard voices in the background.

"Ms. Hill this is detective Murphy. Am I calling at a bad time?"

"These days it feels like any time is a bad time but, no detective, it's not a bad time. Hang on while I turn down the television." A few seconds later she was back on the line. "I hope this is good news."

"We found her."

The shriek caused Murphy to pull the phone from his ear. The shock, joy, relief, and pain all came out in one scream.

"Oh my God! Oh my God! Where is she? Is she alright?"

"She's fine, Ms. Hill. She looks just fine and she's right here in Los Angeles." Murphy could hear Chloe Hill sobbing.

"You said 'we' found her. Who's we?" Chloe said between gulps of air.

"Me, your brother-in-law, and Mr. Maginnes." Murphy had made the decision to credit everyone and place the blame on no one. He felt the most important thing to Chloe Hill was that her daughter was safe. He'd find out the particulars of the situation soon enough.

"Oh my God!" Ms. Hill said again, "Thank you detective. Thank you! Can I talk to her, can I see her?"

"I don't see why not but you might want to wait until morning. There's some paperwork and a lot of information I still need to collect."

"Of course, of course. Oh my God!" she screamed for the third time. "Thank you, Murphy."

"You're welcome Ma'am." He hung up and made two more calls, the first to captain Hill and then to Jeff Giucigiu. He left messages with the good news for both and went back inside. Lyndsay and Teddy, if that was his real name, were putting the finishing touches on a song titled *Pick and Choose.*

"You care to tell me how all this happened?" he said, taking his seat next to Maginnes.

"It's kind of a long story," the P.I. answered.

"Dina says she closes at three."

They ordered another round of drinks and Maginnes told his story. The Readers Digest version was that he had met and fallen in love with Dina. In doing so, he learned of her dream to buy The Bucket, so that became his dream too. They wanted to fix it up, rename it The Six String Saloon, and rebrand it as a place for good, old-fashioned singer songwriters to perform. At Lyndsay's father's request he had been following the girl's career and felt she could one day be one of those singer songwriters. Then she joined Serious Crisis, became a rock star and he felt even more strongly that she could help launch, and be a regular performer at, The Six String. Maybe he could even convince her to bring along DeMaio Turrell once in a while.

"I guess I can understand why you were afraid to say anything to Lyndsay's mother but why didn't you say something to me or to Captain Hill when you had the chance? Put an end to everybody's suffering?" Murphy had a touch of anger in his voice.

"I guess I figured I'd dug myself too deep a hole," Maginnes lamented. "What was I going to say exactly? 'I'm an idiot who's taking advantage of my best friend's daughter to keep alive a fantasy that has little to no chance of success?"

"Something like that."

"Besides, I knew she was safe," he justified.

"Yeah but nobody else did," Murphy scolded.

"Hello again, detective." At some point toward the end of Maginnes's explanation Lyndsay Howlund had approached the bar.

"Miss Howlund," he said shaking her hand, "you have no idea how happy I am to see you again." She smiled. "I like your hair," he added.

"Me too!" Laurence Howlund piped up. "Hey kiddo," he said giving his niece a hug.

"Hi Uncle Larry," she said hugging him right back. "I'm so sorry if I had you all worried." She offered the understatement of the year.

"Mr. Maginnes was just telling us his version of events," Murphy said. "Care to fill us in from your end?" Before Lyndsay answered a handful of people came up to her and told her how good they thought she was. They asked to take a picture with her and she obliged. Then she thanked them as they walked away.

"That's something I just can't wrap my head around. It floors me each and every time. It's weird that people want to take a picture with me."

"I'm pretty sure you're going to have to get used to it," her actor uncle said, "Trust me, it's not that bad."

"Your side of the story, Miss Howlund." Murphy got the conversation back on track, "If you don't mind."

"Several months ago Mags here told me he knew my real Dad," she started. "We got to talking and he mentioned when he first conceived his idea for the club."

Lyndsay told the story of the weird old groupie who became a pseudo uncle and then a trusted confidant. She echoed Maginnes's story about him wanting to buy the L.A. nightclub but added that he was hoping to make it a "Hard Rock Café" kind of experience. Murphy knew she meant the chain of themed restaurants and bars that became popular in the states during the early '80's. Each featured all sorts of music memorabilia and he remembered eating in one of them when he was on Maui.

"I told Mags I could possibly maybe get some stuff from the band to help him get started."

"Why didn't you just ask the guys in the band if you could have an item or two?" Murphy asked what he thought was an obvious question. Then he asked an even more obvious one. "What were you thinking when you just up and left?"

"I wasn't." The quick response told Murphy Murphy she was being completely honest. "I just felt like I wasn't in a good place with the band and you were nosing around."

"Nosing around?" Murphy took offense

"No offense, but you were. I knew I had taken the stuff…"

"Stolen it," the detective interrupted.

"Borrowed it," she answered back, "for Johnny and Dina's bar."

"You say tomato, I say tomahto."

"You do?"

"Actually no, I don't. How about this, you say borrow and I say steal."

"I like the other saying better."

Murphy smiled and thought for a moment about a young girl caught up in circumstances spiraling out of control.

"If you were the one taking the items, why in the world would you mention that to your uncle, the police captain?"

"Guess I outsmarted myself there," she shrugged. "I wanted to get out in front of it, you know tell someone, before Goosh or DeMaio or anyone else did. I thought I could control the situation. I tried to tell my mom that it was no big deal. Nothing serious."

"But she told her brother, your uncle, my captain, and he told me."

"Uh huh. And you, being the consummate professional, took it seriously and proceeded ahead."

Murphy took a couple of deep breaths. He had Lyndsay talking and he feared scolding her about the constant redundancies would derail the conversation.

"So, you said you were in a bad place because I had arrived on the scene."

"Nosing around," she smiled.

"Nosing around," he smiled right back.

"I guess, if I look back in retrospect, I was in a terrible mood. I was worried, disliking the attention and the spotlight more and more." She looked past Murphy like she was remembering exactly how it felt. The detective noticed her uncle staring at her and he saw a slightly sad, knowing, smile cross his face. "Then I got into a fight with Mo Mo and Marty."

"Mr. Kaufmann mentioned that."

"I just wanted to get away, just leave. So I grabbed my guitar, ordered up a zip car, and started driving."

"A what car?"

"A Zip car," she gave him an incredulous look. One that told Murphy she couldn't believe he didn't know what a Zip car was. "It's like a rental, only easier and better."

"Like Uber is to a taxicab?"

"Kinda, sorta, exactly like that."

"So, you drove."

"I did. My proposed plan was to join back up with the band at the next gig but I didn't. I couldn't. I just kept on driving until I got out here. Then I called Mags."

"You didn't think Serious Crisis would be worried about you?"

"Oh, I knew they would be. I picked up my phone and started to attempt a call to Jeff or Walter or my mom a dozen times but I couldn't go through with it." Murphy, Howlund, Maginnes and Dina were all listening now. "I guess I couldn't get past the fear that they might be angry at me to comprehend the thought that they would be worried about me." Murphy surveyed the group and noticed a tear roll down Dina's right cheek. "Do you think they'll forgive me detective? Are you going to arrest me?"

"Yes and no," Murphy assured her, "but I think Herbie wants his whip back."

"I'll buy him a brand new, better one," Maginnes offered.

"So, where do we go from here?" It was the actor clearly sensing the scene coming to an end. Murphy thought for a moment.

"I go back home. Lyndsay talks to her mother before hopping on a plane and rejoining Serious Crisis, and the two of you," he pointed at Maginnes and Howlund, "go back to doing whatever it is you do on a daily basis."

"Maybe we can agree to connect together on this day, at this place, every year to commemorate our partnership," Maginnes suggested." An annual anniversary of sorts." He smiled.

"Don't count on it," Murphy said getting up. "Now, if you don't mind Mr. Howlund, could you please give me a lift back to my rental car. I still may be able to catch a redeye out of here tonight."

"No problem," the actor said. "Why don't you follow us to my place Lyndsay? You can crash there tonight and I'd love to catch up."

"Sound good Unc," she agreed, "and I'll catch you later Mags." She kissed the private investigator on the cheek.

"Just let me pay the tab," Murphy said, raising his right hand to get Dina's attention. For the second time that evening Johnny "Jack" Maginnes used his own hand to stop Murphy's action.

"Don't be silly, detective," he said. "This one's on the house."

Murphy arrived at the airport in plenty of time to give Charlie Carlucci a call.

"I'm headed home," he said, hoping she could hear the smile in his voice.

"What did you say?" she practically screamed over the background noise at The Gas Pump Lounge. Murphy guessed she couldn't hear the smile in his voice.

"Busy night?" he said louder than he would have liked.

"Just another Friday," Charlie said. Murphy could hear the smile in her voice.

"I'm on my way home," he said again.

"That's fantastic news!" she yelled, "Feel like a mountain getaway this weekend?"

"You do, or do I?" he asked

"Both silly. God you're cute."

"How can I say no to that?"

"You can't," she said and hung up.

At that moment Laurence and Lyndsay Howlund were inside the actor's Hollywood Hills home. He pulled the cork on a bottle of Woodford Reserve Double Batch and poured them both a glass. His is a bit fuller than hers.

"How do you deal with all the attention, the screaming fans, the fame?" she asked her uncle.

"First by realizing I'm not famous." He held up his glass to toast his niece, then took a gulp. She drank too.

"But you've been in so many movies, television shows, commercials. People love you. They know who you are."

"That's sweet of you to say Lyndsay but think about it," he took another drink. "There are almost eight *billion* people on this planet. Nearly three hundred and twenty five million of them in this country alone. I'm just one. You're just one. Clooney is famous, Brad Pitt is famous, Bono is famous. I'm just a guy who loves what he does and is lucky enough to get to keep doing it."

"But I grew up watching all those people around mom. They could be so mean, so nasty. They thought they were so much more important than her." She took another sip of bourbon. "They made her cry. She didn't think I knew, since she wouldn't do it in front of me, but I heard her. In her room late at night. Crying."

The actor thought about that for a long moment. It made him wonder if he had been too hard on his sister-in-law.

"You aren't like them," he said to his niece, "and you don't have to turn into them regardless of how many Grammys you win or albums and tickets you sell. You can be popular or famous and still be a good person, a decent human being."

"Can you?" she wondered honestly.

"I believe you can." He poured each of them a little more bourbon and they drank in silence for a few minutes.

"Do you love it?" Laurence Howlund asked.

"The Woodford?"

"No silly, the music? The art?"

"More than anything."

"Remember our 'what if' game?"

"Of course."

"Well then *what if* you decided it was okay to keep all that love just for yourself?"

A Few Brief Summaries

DeMaio Turrell stood on stage in front of ten thousand screaming, lighter holding fans.

"And last but not least, on keyboards, guitars, and vocals, the heart and soul of Serious Crisis.... Lyndsay "Stray Dog" Howlund!" The audience roared with applause. It came from everywhere and lasted several minutes. Big Joe Lionns, Herbie Albanese, Chuckie Gruber and DeMaio Turrell applauded with them. So did Jeffery Giucigiu, Mo Morrisey, Smitty, Jimmy Dimsum, Olive Green and Marty Kaufmann. Lyndsay Howlund raised her arms, smiled her biggest, most sincere smile, and soaked it all in.

Johnny "Jack" Maginnes sat holding hands with Dina Feinstein. Across the desk a First Community bank loan officer tapped out some keys on a computer. Maginnes smiled a nervous smile at Dina who squeezed his hand as a response.

"Tell me one more time what you're going to call the place if, and it's still a big if, this loan goes through?" the banker pushed his glasses farther up the bridge of his nose.

"The Six String Saloon," Maginnes said proudly.

"I like it," the banker said. "Oh, here's Doris now." A slender woman reached past Maginnes's left shoulder and handed the banker a manila folder. He thanked her and started to read. Before leaving Doris gave Dina a small smile. "Well," the banker leaned back in his chair and put his hands behind his head. Maginnes thought he looked relaxed, maybe even a little smug. His own stomach was churning. "It appears everything is in order folks and this loan can advance forward," he smiled. "Congratulations and good luck with The Six String Saloon."

Judith Colman got to work half an hour early. She tried to every day. That way she could make sure the place was ready for customers and it gave her a chance to get the dogs settled before she opened Bar Flight to the public. She always parked in the back, in a space at the far corner of the lot. One reason was because she didn't want to take up a prime customer space and the other reason was it was directly under a streetlamp. She liked the security of walking to her car, under the light, with the dogs. She locked up and then walked around the building to the front door. Leaning against it was a large FedEx box addressed to her. She picked it up easily, since it didn't weigh much, and she was pretty strong if she did say so herself. She locked the door behind her, Namath and

Bear, and took the package to the bar where she cut it open and pulled out the contents. Secured in bubble wrap she found a framed *Eddie and the Cruisers* movie poster and a brand new DVD copy of the film. She removed the poster from the protective packaging and gave it a good, hard look. She smiled. In the bottom left corner someone had written something. She read it out loud.

"Judith, tell "The Pizzer" *Eddie and The Cruisers* are here!" It was signed "XOXO, Sal". Judith knew the line by heart. It was what Sal Amato said to Frank Ridgeway when the band showed up at a Somer's Point, New Jersey club called Tony Mart's. Murphy had gotten her the autograph.

Captain Dave Hill directed the tow truck driver like a member of the ground crew at O'Hare International.

"That's good right there, Ginger!" he called out. The driver's name was Will Baker but everybody called him Ginger because he had a bushy red beard and constantly blasted Cream from the cassette tape player in the truck. He put the truck in park and climbed out of the cab. The rig's engine idled, the song Badge blared on.
"That the one?" Ginger pointed to a yellow Renault.

"That's an affirmative yes," Hill nodded.

"Are we junking it?"

"Nah," he shook his head, "let's donate it to charity. Cars for Kids or the Humane Society, you choose. And Ginger?"

"Yeah Cap?"

"Have your guys paint it first. Get rid of the ridiculous writing on the side."

"You got it," he said and started hooking up the Le Car.

"Dud" Hill went back inside the precinct and into his office. He picked up his phone and punched out a few numbers.

"Motor pool," the voice on the other end said.

"This is Captain Hill. Have someone bring the new Taurus over to the precinct. One of my top detectives will be expecting it today," he said, knowing the new car would come as a complete surprise to Murphy. Laurence Howlund was soaking in the Southern California sun, sitting by his pool in the backyard of his Hollywood Hills home. He leafed through a script he had received, unsolicited, by messenger that morning. On the ground by his feet were two separate offers to serve as a commercial spokesperson. One for a mattress company, the other for adult male diapers. The phone, on a towel at the end of his chaise lounge rang and he answered it.

"Did you get the script I sent over?" To Howlund's surprise the voice belonged to his sister-in-law Chloe Hill.

"This came from you?" he was bewildered.

"It did," she confirmed. "Read it. I think you'd be perfect for the Mitchy role."

"Okay, I'll take a look," he paused, "By the way, who's directing?"

"Hanks," she said and hung up.

Murphy Murphy grabbed the bowl of fresh, steaming popcorn. He brought it into the living room and plopped down on the couch next to Charlie Carlucci. He set the bowl on the coffee table and popped a couple of kernels into his mouth. He put his right hand on Charlie's thigh and grabbed the remote with his left. He turned on the TV.

"TV tonight?" She asked, "No Mozart?"

"Neither," he said smiling, "I have a surprise."

He pushed a couple of buttons on the remote and the screen came to life. A drum roll preceded an orchestral fanfare and a black and white, Twentieth Century Fox, logo appeared. Three of five spotlights moved back and forth. The next image told Murphy and Charlie that what they were about to see was "A CinemaScope Picture" as the orchestra concluded its famous Alfred Newman theme. The screen dipped to black then faded up on scene one. Someone drives up to a gas station in an old, beat up sedan. The driver exits the car. It's Paul Newman as "Fast" Eddie Felson. Murphy and Charlie settled into the couch to watch *The Hustler*.

AND SO THE STORY REACHES ITS CONCLUSION AND ENDS

ACKNOWLEDGEMENTS
AND RECOGNITION

I had a ton of fun writing this book and hope you enjoyed reading it. As with my previous work I have several people to thank.

It all starts with Sarah. Thank you for the encouragement and inspiration and for the gift of time to dream, ponder, procrastinate, formulate and write. I put every word on paper with the hope that you'll like it.

Jake Hirshland once again took time out of his incredibly busy and successful life as a member of the rock band, Post Animal, to make spelling, punctuation and, grammar corrections. He also lobbed in ideas and enhancements, especially when it came to the particulars of life on the road for a rock and roll musician. I could have written this without him but why?

I always have a few folks read what I write before the book is made available to you. To Susan Green, Daisy Phipps, and David Kamens I offer my heartfelt thanks for your time, energy, suggestions, and corrections. To a person they said it was my best work yet. Well actually only one of them said it but it still meant the world to me.

Matthew Laurance also read this when it was 8 x 10 sheets in a binder but he contributed so much more than that. Thanks pal.

Everything in this book happened. In my head. The characters are just that and any resemblance to real persons (living or dead) is purely coincidental. Like most authors my characters need names. Some in this work are made of whole cloth while others are eerily similar to friends, relatives and former colleagues. Those folks were all kind enough to say it was okay. I hope I did you proud.

Finally, my deepest appreciation to Bobby Collins and the team at Beacon Publishing Group. I am thrilled to be part of the team and pinch myself everyday knowing you have faith in my work.

Until next time.